For the people who run toward the fire.

marks on the moon

T.D. COLBERT

MARKS ON THE MOON

Book One, Night & Day Duet

Copyright © 2022 T.D. Colbert

Published: T.D. Colbert 2022

Editing: Jenn Lockwood Editing

Sensitivity Editing: Renita McKinney, A Book A Day Author Services

Cover Design: T.D. Colbert

www.tdcolbert.com

prologue

STEVIE

MY HUSBAND ISN'T *in love with me.*

I've always known that, for as long as we both shall live, he'd stand by me.

But that was before the diagnosis. Before we knew about the disease that will wreak havoc on his body, tearing him apart slowly.

He gave me "till death do us part." But now, death's knocking.

And he wants her.

The craziest part is, I'm going to be the one who brings her back to him.

This is the story of my husband and the love of his life.

But the love of his life isn't me.

present day

28 + 40 YEARS

CHAPTER ONE

tess

WHEN I GOT THE CALL, I had just finished scrubbing blood off my hands.

A three-car pile-up. A couple of kids drag racing.

My favorite shifts to work are the night shifts, when the rest of the world is asleep. But some nights, like tonight, when I helped intubate a seventeen-year-old, I'm reminded why so many people steer clear of this line of work.

It takes a toll on you, and sometimes, you don't even realize it until it's too late. Until the scars it leaves on you are worse than any you've sewn up on someone else.

I know I got into nursing because of my dad. He always said I was meant for it. I had spent my childhood hearing stories of him braving the worst to save other people, and it became the norm for me. You don't sleep until the world as you know it is as safe as it can be.

"Hey." Annie pokes her head into the bathroom,

with Alexa right behind her. I'm re-tying my cap and straightening myself out. "You good? That was a rough one."

Annie and Alexa are my two very best friends in the world. We all started at the hospital within a year of each other, and we have been through the wringer. Those trauma bonds, man. They tie you to a person.

It's rare that the three of us all work a shift together, but we live together in an apartment a few miles away from the hospital, so we're together a lot. We leave snacks in each other's lockers and bring coffee when it's the only lifeline we have. Tonight, it was supposed to just be Annie and me, but Alexa ended up covering for someone else. We all look at ourselves in the mirror, our faces drained of color and any sign of life, wisps of untamed cap hair shooting out from the sides of our heads. I turn to them slowly and nod.

"Tomorrow will be another day," I say, walking through them and heading back down the hallway.

"Yeah, but you'll be sleeping most of the day," Alexa calls after me. They both start walking with me. "It's okay to take a minute if you need to, ya know."

Alexa is the sweet one. She's concerned for everyone's well-being, she listens to what I don't say, and she knows my Starbucks order by heart.

"They don't pay us enough for this shit," Annie says, pulling her long brown hair into a messy bun. "They really don't."

Annie is the, um, *direct* one. She is a damn good nurse, an even better friend, and she gets shit done.

And me, I'm somewhere between them. I care way

more than a healthy amount, but I keep trucking. Because I'm Jack Connor's daughter, and that's what we do.

I look at the clock as I'm walking down the hallway back to the main triage area. I've only been working for one hour and three minutes, but it feels like I've been here for days. Only ten hours and fifty-seven minutes to go. But just as I'm turning into the triage area, my phone buzzes wildly in my scrub pocket.

"I'll see you guys back in there," I say, and they nod and walk by me. I pause and lean back against the wall to pull it out. My supervisor, Marie, had told me to take five after the intubation, but I hardly ever take the whole break. I can't. I'm a nurse manager now, and I know people are counting on me. They're counting on me to keep on keepin' on, even when we have nothing left in the tank. No time for breaks. There's too much to be done.

But when I look down at my phone screen, I freeze when I see the area code.

It's someone from home.

I click the green button and hold the phone to my ear.

"Hello, this is Tess," I say.

There's a pause.

"Hello?" I ask again.

A woman clears her throat on the other end.

"Tess, hi. It's been a long time," she says. I don't recognize the voice. "This is Stevie. Stevie Waters."

My mouth goes dry, my stomach immediately knots,

and I swear my heart stops for a beat. I don't say anything. My breaths are shallow in my lungs.

"I'm sorry to call you like this, but..." Her voice trails off for a minute, and I realize she's crying.

"Stevie..." I say quietly, pushing her to finish.

"Cade has melanoma. We found out last week that it's stage three. It's not good. But he...I know he...he wants to see you. Can you come?" Her voice cracks a little as she asks.

Now my heart is making up for those beats it skipped, because it feels like it's pounding so hard that it's going to burst out of my chest.

I brace myself against the wall as I grow light-headed. I feel the panic attack taking over my body. My feet start to tingle as the blood drains from my extremities.

"Tess?"

I swallow and force out a slow breath.

"Yes, I can come."

CHAPTER TWO

cade

KNOWING you're going to die but feeling perfectly fine is weird.

In theory, you know the end is coming, but there are no signs of it.

I've thought a lot the last few days about what would have happened if I had never gone to the dermatologist. Stevie had been begging me to get this spot on my leg checked for over a year. I told her it was probably an old burn scar. Nothing to worry about. Or my go-to, "Black people don't get skin cancer." Joke's on me, I guess. And I know Grannie would be so pissed at me for even joking about it.

I finally went, just knowing everything would be okay. I run into burning buildings for a living. I've known unfathomable loss. I'm always gonna be okay.

I haven't said much to Stevie—or to anyone—since I got the news last week. Dr. Sang sat Stevie and me down. Stage-three melanoma. That's a fancy way of saying that it's already spread to some of my lymph nodes. Dr. Sang laid out all the options—and I do mean all of them. First and foremost, have the spot removed. Then, remove the affected lymph nodes and assess if the cancer is anywhere else. If it's still there, I can do radiation, immunotherapy, chemo, clinical trials...

It all just sounds like a bunch of ways to make whatever is left of my life as miserable as possible. And the best part is that Doc says that even if we get it all on the first go-round, I have a high chance of it coming back. I told them I'd think about what I wanted to do. I know Stevie is dying for me to make a decision, but I just can't. I don't want to. I wish I had never gone in the first place, lived out the rest of my days blissfully ignorant.

I'm officially on medical leave from the station, which is fucking killing me. So, I'm focusing on other things. Things I can still do. Things I can still fix. Like the faucet that leaks in the mudroom. The bottom step that sags out on the front porch. Stevie's a machine. She's running shit like she normally does: calling people, making freezer meals, getting laundry done. Anything she can do to keep herself busy.

I know there's so much I should be thinking about: making sure my will is in order, making sure all is set with my insurance so Stevie will be okay...saying my goodbyes.

But somehow, for the last few nights, when I lie awake and stare out the window in front of me into the dark woods, all I can see is her face. Tess.

I think about dying. I think about leaving this Earth,

saying all my goodbyes, and not getting to say mine to her.

And it hurts more than I know this cancer will.

I'm outside a few hours later, hammering away at the front porch step, pulling up the old, rusted nails and throwing them in my tool tray as I lay out the fresh new plank. I run my hand over the cedar and inhale. This is one thing I'll miss. The smell of fresh-cut wood.

It's hot out for September. I'm more of a cold-weather guy. I don't like feeling like I'm baking. Ironic that skin cancer from sunlight is probably going to be what takes me out.

I push the sleeves of my shirt up, letting my tattoos out into the light. I'm breaking a sweat on my brow, and I swipe a bead away when I hear a car rolling up our long driveway through the trees. I figure it's my mother-in-law or one of the guys from the station. Cindy has been here at least three times since last week, dropping off food and checking in on us. She hasn't been the most attentive mother in the past, but she does tend to show up when the going gets tough. The thing is, her years of neglecting to recognize when Stevie needed her made Stevie tough. Now, Cindy tries to show up, but Stevie doesn't need her.

I push myself up off the ground and spin around to the top of the driveway just as the car is parking. It's a silver sedan of some sort that I don't recognize. And then the door opens, and I feel all the air shoot out of my lungs, like someone punched me in the stomach. She gets out slowly and closes the door behind her, our eyes locked on one another, and I take her in in complete silence for just a second.

Long and lean like she always was, with a little more curve in some spots. Her long, copper hair is still as wispy as ever, cascading down to the middle of her ribs. Her jaw is tight as she narrows those emerald eyes at me, those lips that I've seen in my sleep in a perfect line. Her jeans hug hips I'm still not used to, and though she's changed a little, I still feel like I know her better than I've ever known another person. After another beat, her lips curve up into the faintest smile, and I feel my body go weak.

"Hey, Bobby Brown," she says, and I can't help but crack a smile. She will never let me live down my love for New Edition. And that's okay, because I will go to my grave being their most loyal fan.

"Hey, Boss," I say back, and I see her swallow as she takes in the nickname. "What in the hell are you—"

"I called her," I hear my wife say, and my spine goes straight as I turn to look up at her at the top of the porch steps. "Hi, Tess. Thank you for making the trip. Come on in."

She smiles, but I know my wife. And I know she'd rather be doing anything than smiling in this moment. Tess clears her throat and tightens her purse strap on her shoulder as she walks up the path and up the steps. Just as her foot reaches for the first one, I instinctively reach out and grab her elbow.

"Watch that first one, there," I say. "I'm putting a

new plank in, and we all know you're not good on your feet. Can't have you falling right when you get here."

She shoots daggers with her eyes, but her lips curve into that amazing smile again.

"We both know I'm gonna trip—at least twice," she says, and my eyes widen as I laugh at yet another inside joke. I sit for a moment in how easy it is to fall right back into place with her.

I follow her up the steps and into the foyer, where Stevie is instructing her to hang her scarf and purse.

"Guess it's a little colder up north, huh?" Stevie asks, her charm turned all the way up. Stevie is a lot of things, and the perfect hostess is one of them.

"Yeah, it's definitely colder than here. Guess I didn't need this," Tess says, tugging the scarf off her neck, and I freeze when I see it. The purple-and-blue-striped scarf I had given her the day after her father died. The one my grandmother made her.

"I've seen that before," I say, nodding to it. She nods her head and clears her throat, then lifts her eyes to Stevie. But Stevie doesn't ask for an explanation. She just smiles faintly and leads us into the kitchen.

She grabs a bowl of chips from the counter and pulls some salsa out of the fridge.

"There's more salsa in here," she says, "and some wine on the rack. I'm going to head out and let you two catch up." She turns to Tess, who is standing awkwardly in the corner of the kitchen. "Thank you again for coming." Then, she turns to me. "I'll see you for dinner."

The smile runs away from her face as quickly as she

13

forced it there, and she brushes past me and toward the door. I turn back to Tess.

"Have a seat. I'll be right back," I tell her. I jog to catch up with Stevie in the driveway before she opens her door. "Steve," I call to her.

She turns to me, her big blue eyes looking up into mine, filled with so much despair that I can hardly handle it.

"Steve...what's going on? How did you...why did you..." I start to ask her all the questions flying through my head, but per usual, she already knows what I'm trying to say before I get it out.

"You fell asleep the other night and had something in your hand. When I went to pull it out, I realized it was that photo you used to have in your truck mirror. That one of her and you, with the nursing pin in it. I've seen you hold it from time to time through the years. You don't talk about her much, but the way you look at the picture says a lot. And the fact that it's something you held onto when you found out you could be..." She refuses to say the word "dying" out loud. She clears her throat. "You don't ever bring her up, but the look on your face when the rest of the guys at the station do...it says a lot."

My eyes drop in shame. I should have put it away.

"But, why..." I start to say again.

"Look," Stevie says, "I have no idea what really happened between you two. What she was to you, or what she...what she might still be to you. I just know that I have absolutely *no* clue what you're going through right now. And I also know that you want to see her, whether you admit it or not. So, I got her number from Dirk and called her on Wednesday, asked her to come down."

There's a long pause.

"Stevie, I…" I feel like an asshole for not being able to mumble more than a few syllables, but I really have no idea what to say. I *did* want to see Tess. But the look on my wife's face makes me wish the cancer would take me sooner. "Thank you. Truly. You should stay with us. You'd love her."

She forces a lightning-speed smile as she tugs her door open.

"I'm sure I would," she says before she gets in her car and closes the door. I watch as she turns the car around and disappears into the trees. I suck in a long breath and walk back up the porch steps to where Tess Connor is waiting for me in my house.

When I turn back into the kitchen, I stop at the sight of her. She's sitting at the table, her long hair sliding off her shoulder in front of her as she rubs the belly of Buster, our ten-year-old golden retriever. She smiles at him as his tongue flops out of his mouth, and I walk through the doorway toward her. And I notice, as we get closer, her naked ring finger.

"He'll do anything for a good belly rub," I say, opening the fridge and taking out the pitcher of iced tea I made yesterday. "He and I have that in common."

She smiles and shakes her head.

I hold the pitcher up.

"Tea?" I ask. She smiles again.

"Have you ever known me to turn it down?"

"Not once," I say. "Tea for T."

She rolls her eyes. "How'd I know that was coming?"

I laugh and bring two glasses to the table, pulling out the chair next to her.

A breeze blows through the window behind her, and I get a whiff of her so strong it makes my whole body stiffen. It's crazy how just a simple scent or a glass of unsweetened iced tea can take you back to a whole different place and time in your life. To an exact moment that seemed so small at the time but became one of those ones that shifted everything.

"So," I say, "tell me what I missed over the last five years."

thirteen years ago

15 + 27 YEARS

CHAPTER THREE

tess

"YOU COMING OUT WITH US, CONNOR?" Tate asks right when the game clock runs out and the cheerleaders storm the field.

"Yeah, come out, Tess," Mina says, pretending to be more into me coming than she is about Tate noticing her. She's been my friend for years but more out of convenience for her, I think. We've lived three doors down from each other since we were six. She has a single mom. I have a single dad. So, over the years, our parents relied on each other for pick-ups and drop-offs.

And before you ask, yes, we did attempt to *Parent Trap* them when we were in seventh grade. We set up a date for them in Mina's living room, complete with a flashlight-lit dinner on TV tables with "The Way You Look Tonight" playing in the background off of Mina's iPod Nano. They humored us and ate their ramen noodles and toaster-oven garlic bread together, but afterward, they explained to us that they were just friends.

Mina is on the girls' tennis team at school, and Tate is one of those default popular kids. He's friends with all the jocks, so ipso facto, he's popular regardless of what he wears or what his extracurricular life looks like. It also doesn't hurt that his parents have money and are rarely home. Mina's been in love with him since we started high school, and I wish he would freakin' notice. She's a damn catch, seriously. Long blonde hair, bright-blue eyes, and long legs to boot. She could wear a trash bag and it would look amazing. Tennis isn't the typical all-star sport in high school, but Mina is pretty good. She made it to states her freshman year and is on track to do it again this year. She's already been scouted by some college coaches, so people pay attention to her.

I look down at my phone, and I smile. A text from Dad.

All done, kiddo. Headed to Andy's. Come say hi to your old man.

I look back up and shake my head, holding my phone up.

"My dad's shift is over," I say, "and I told him I'd meet him for a bite to eat. Y'all go ahead and have fun."

"You like hangin' out with those old dudes, huh?" Tate asks. And I whip my head back around to him. I should take offense to it, but I shrug it off and smile.

"They're a lot more fun," I say as I turn back around and walk down the bleachers. It's the truth. Mina's my friend—probably the best one I have—but aside from a few other people I've been close with throughout my school years, I don't have many others. My favorite people to be around are my dad and the guys from the station.

My favorite human in the world is my pops. My mom died three days after giving birth to me, so the two of us is all that I know. They said she had somehow gotten an infection during delivery that got into her bloodstream. Before the doctors could figure out what was wrong, her organs had failed within forty-eight hours. Before that, the doctors had told her it was her hormones and that she was being dramatic.

That's why I'll be a nurse someday.

Because no matter what anyone's going through, whether it's organ failure or a splinter in their thumb, they deserve better than what my mom got.

I think about my poor pops a lot when I think about my mom dying. About how scared he must have been, just getting started as a parent and having to do it on his own, all the while saying goodbye to the other half of him.

He says I was Mom's final gift to him. We look freakishly alike: same auburn hair, same green eyes. And from what people tell me, our mannerisms are the same, too. If I could say one thing to her, I'd thank her for choosing him to be my dad. They don't make them like him anymore.

I text him back as I walk out of the stadium and up the hill toward the traffic light.

On my way.

My favorite nights are spent with Dad and the guys, listening to their tales of the shifts, listening to them talk about their most impressive plays during their old softball days. Most of them have worked at the station together for at least twenty years. Most of them were around when my mom died. Most of them were at my first birthday party. Some of them have picked me up from school when Dad couldn't make it. They all take their roles in my life seriously, and I know I wouldn't be the girl I am without them. It's a little unorthodox, I guess, for a teenage girl to prefer a bunch of thirty- and forty-something firemen for company than people her own age. But I know where I feel most at home, and it's with those guys. I like to keep my eye on them. Make sure they're eating. Make sure, if they drink too much, that someone gets them home. Make sure my dad smiles now and then.

I cross Main Street and walk a few more blocks until I reach Andy's, Dad and the guys' favorite bar that just happens to be across the street from the Dalesville Fire Station. When I open the door and the little bell jingles, I hear the roar of eight men chanting my name and holding their arms out, and I smile. I make my rounds, giving them all hugs and taking the open chair next to my dad. Rose, the waitress who's been working here for as long as the bar's been open, comes right to the table. She can't be more than five feet tall, with curly black hair and dark-brown eyes. She's probably a few years older than my dad, but working in this bar has aged her.

"Hi, sweetie pie," she says. "Curly fries and a root beer. Anything else?"

I smile and shake my head.

"You know me so well, Rose," I say. She winks as

21

she sets another pitcher of beer down in the center of the table. "So, how was shift tonight?" I ask. Dad nods, and I let out a sigh of relief. That usually means it was manageable. Not much to report. Just then, the bell rings again, and to my surprise, the guys start their welcome cheer yet again. I look up, confused. I should have been the last one coming for our group.

And that's when I see him for the first time.

Tall, with big, broad shoulders. He has on a white t-shirt and khakis, like the rest of the guys, but his shirt stretches tighter around his arms. From either direction, I see his tattoos spilling out of the collar and the sleeves of the cotton, running halfway down his right arm and all the way down the left. His skin is a light brown, and he has jet-black hair that's cut real short. His beard is trimmed to the nines, and when he smiles, I swear there's a spark in the room. He's scanning the table, nodding in each guy's direction, until his eyes meet mine. Big and brown, with some streaks of goldish yellow in them, like they're swirling with bourbon. He pauses for a moment, then nods in my direction, too.

I nod back and turn to my dad for an explanation.

"Glad you made it, man," Dad says. Rich reaches to his side and grabs a chair from the table next to him, sliding it over to ours. "Have a seat."

"Thanks, guys," the new guy says, pulling the chair out and taking a seat. He drops his keys and wallet on the table.

"Cade, this is my daughter, Tess," Dad says, putting

his arm around me. "Honey, this is Cade. This has been his first week at the station."

"Hi, Tess," he says, flashing that same smile that makes my stomach flutter and burn deep down. I don't remember my name ever sounding this good in all my life.

"I didn't know the station was getting a new guy," I say. "Nice to meet you."

"From what I hear, you're the *actual* boss," he says with another killer smile. My dad chuckles and nudges me.

"Don't give her a big head. These jackasses already let her think she runs the world," he says, his belly bouncing as he laughs, and I can't help but smile.

"'Think?'" I say. "They just know the truth."

The rest of the night carries on like normal. Rose bringing endless pitchers of beer and baskets of curly fries. The guys eating their weight in bar food, shaking off the week. The ones that are married talking about their wives and kids, the single ones talking about dates or cars. But I can't sit back and relax like normal, because there's a tall, dark, and holy-shit handsome stranger sitting a few feet away from me that's shaking up my normal. I can't keep my eyes off him for more than a few seconds at a time. I watch everything about him. The way he really looks at whoever is talking. The way he smiles at Rose every time he asks for something or she brings something to the table. The way the whole room seems to rumble when his laughter booms through it. The way the veins in his arms snake up, bubbling under his tattoos and making me salivate.

Jesus Christ, Tess. He's, like, old. And he works with your father.

But those gold streaks in his eyes. And those lips. And that perfectly groomed beard…

I can't remember the last time there's been a Black firefighter around here. Maybe never. My dad used to say that, when they first moved to Dalesville a few years before I was born, my mom came home from the store one day crying. She told my dad they needed to move. When he asked her why, she said that it was too white. She had been in town for months and had seen one person of color, and it bothered her. She and Dad grew up about thirty miles south of Dalesville, closer to D.C. Things were much more diverse, much more multicultural. But the thing was, they couldn't really afford to live anywhere else. Dalesville is a small farm town. He promised her if things hadn't gotten better by the time their first kid was school-age, he would do whatever he had to do to move. But then my mom died, and by the time I was ready for school, my dad relied heavily on people in the community. He had gotten Captain, was making enough money to support us without Mom, and knew we had to stay.

Truth be told, Dalesville has gotten much more diverse as the years have gone on, but it could definitely stand to be less white-washed. It's one of the reasons that I plan to work at some big-city hospital one day.

My dad is paying the bill—paying for everyone like he usually does at the end of every month—and we're all scooting out from the booths and chairs that are

24

crowded into the corner that the whole town seems to save for us. I'm standing by the door, waiting for Rose to bring the check back, when Cade makes his way to me.

"Well," he says, tucking his wallet back in his pocket after my dad refused to let him pay, "it was nice to finally meet the one who keeps all these guys in line. Hope I don't add too much trouble to your plate."

I swallow and smile.

"I can handle it," I tell him. "Years of experience."

He smiles back as he pushes the door open.

"Somehow, I have no doubt. Night, Tess."

CHAPTER FOUR

cade

IT'S BEEN a few weeks since I started at the Dalesville station, and I'm settling in quite nicely. I'm about twenty years younger than most of the other guys, but I'm fitting in fine, especially with Chief. I love the shifts we work together, if for nothing else than his stories.

I've learned a lot about him over the last few weeks. I've learned a lot about his daughter, too. Her mom died a few days after having her from sepsis, and the poor guy was left in a new town with a newborn. But as he says, "It takes a village, and that's just what we got." The guys at the station and their wives and families stepped up to help with meals and finding babysitters when Tess was little. His sister, Marie, temporarily moved to Dalesville for a short time to help around the house while he was getting the hang of things. Apparently, she fell for some guy in town, and it went sour, so she couldn't wait to get back to Massachusetts as fast as possible when Chief felt like he could do it on his own.

Since then, though, with some intermittent help, it's just been Chief and Tess. And it seems like she's really taken the reins.

The girl shows up to the station at least three times a week, despite being a busy teenager, to bring me leftovers or some sort of baked good. Last week, she came by at ten at night on a school night because Chief forgot his blood pressure medication. She can't drive yet, so she rides her bike or gets a ride with one of the older kids from school. I guess Chief has a lot of trust in the town, but more than a few times, I've offered to run her back home. I don't like the thought of her being out at night by herself.

I still don't fully get why she wants to spend so much time around us old guys, but I have to admit, it's fun having her around. She's the little mama of the station, even with Mel there to keep us all in line, but when she knows all her ducks are in a row—and by ducks, I mean us—she loosens up. She smiles, she laughs, she gives the guys shit. She's special. She's one of those people you can watch for a few minutes, and you just know they are meant for something big. I'm not sure what her something big is, but I know she's going to kick its ass. She has Chief's unmatchable work ethic, but she takes it a step further.

I have the night off—the first time I've had a Friday off in a while. Just as I'm about to dial up some of my buddies from Dilly's, the bar I used to tend at a few nights a week, my phone rings on my kitchen table. It's Chief.

"Hey, Chief," I say. "Something wrong? Need me to come in?"

"Nope," he says. "I'm off this evening, too. Wanted to see if you wanted to join some of the fellas and me for a poker game. We're gonna head up to the Dalesville game for a bit and probably come back to my place around halftime to start playing."

I think about it. I haven't been to a high school football game in a long time—probably since I last played in one. Dalesville was our rival in Grantstown, the small town I'm from about five miles west. I was a linebacker, and I wasn't half bad. Made it to the select state tournament one year. My mom came.

"Who they playin'?" I ask. He chuckles.

"Your beloved Grantstown Gators," he says. "Thought you might want to come watch them get their asses kicked by Dalesville for the third year in a row."

I scoff.

"Ha! I've never been to a Dalesville-Grantstown game where Dalesville came out winning. I'm the Gators' good-luck charm. I'm in," I tell him.

"Uh-oh," he says with another laugh. "Cool. See you there. Game's at six."

"See ya."

A few hours later, I'm decked out in my favorite Grantstown hoodie and a pair of basketball shorts, ready to be as obnoxious as I can be amongst a crowd full of the enemy. I pay at the gate and head inside, walking toward the home bleachers. I pass by an alleyway between the school building and an equipment shed, and that's when I see her.

Long, brownish hair with those streaks of copper that are especially noticeable under the fluorescent stadium lights. She's got skinny jeans on and a pair of black Chuck Taylors, with a vintage "Dalesville Fire Dept." hoodie on. I smile.

Always reppin'.

I watch her for the briefest moment. She's leaning against the brick of the school building, chewing on her thumb, while a girl next to her talks loudly to the crowd of kids around them. I watch as she scans all their faces, like she's trying to decipher what it is they're thinking or feeling. She laughs only when they laugh. She smiles only when they smile.

It's like she can't be content until she knows every other soul around her is.

I watch her blankly for another moment. But then, she catches me.

Her face lights up when she sees me, and it makes my stomach flip.

There's something about this girl feeling joy that makes me feel happier than I can remember feeling in a long time.

She excuses herself from the group of kids, who hardly seem to notice, and makes her way through the crowd to me. She gives me a side-hug, and I squeeze her shoulder.

"They got you to come, huh?" she says with a smile.

"'Course. I couldn't let them watch my Gators destroy y'all without me," I say with a devious smile. She widens her eyes and drops her jaw.

"We will just see, won't we," she says. I shrug.

"You like football?"

She thinks about it for a minute, as if it's a hard question to answer. Then, she looks up at me and smiles.

"Actually, no," she says with a laugh. "I find it incredibly boring. And honestly, I couldn't give two shits who wins this game tonight."

I feel a smile break out over my face.

"Fair enough," I tell her. Then, I lean down to her ear. "In that case, root for the Gators, would ya?"

She steps back and puts a hand to her chest, feigning shock.

"I could *never*," she says with a fake gasp that makes me laugh. "I *bleed* green and white, sir. Dalesville for*ever!*"

Just then, the girl with the voice that carries seemingly across the stadium calls her name and waves her over.

"Looks like you've been summoned," I tell her. "I'll see ya later?"

She nods, but I can't help but notice that her face drops a little.

"Yeah, I'll make sure the kitchen is stocked for tonight's card game," she says. "See ya."

. . .

About an hour or so later, it's halftime, and Chief and the other guys are leaving. My Gators are blowing out the Dalesville Ducks, and half the stadium has cleared.

"Tess riding home with you?" I ask Chief as we make our way to the parking lot. He shakes his head.

"Supposedly, she's going to a friend's tonight," he says with an eye roll, like he doesn't believe it. Huh. Never would have pegged Tess to be a rebellious teenager who lies to her dad.

"Uh-oh," I chuckle. "She testing the waters?"

He shakes his head again.

"I wish," he says. I shoot him a curious look. "Not that I want her in any kind of trouble. But I just wish the girl would let herself have some fun. She studies so hard. She practically takes care of the house herself when I'm at work. And then she comes to the station and takes care of shit there." He pauses for a minute as we get to the aisle between our trucks. "Sometimes I feel like I've failed her."

I look at him thoughtfully for a moment.

"Well, I know I haven't been around long yet, Chief," I say, "but it's pretty easy to tell how much that girl adores you. That doesn't seem like a failure to me."

He thinks about my words for a moment, then nods slowly.

"See ya at the house, Waters."

I turn to where I parked my truck, or where I *think* I parked my truck, only to realize it isn't there. I see it two aisles over and start weaving through slowly moving cars and trucks and teenagers to get to it. Just as I reach it, I hear my name.

31

"Cade! Wait!"

I turn to see Tess running through the crowd.

She finally gets to me, out of breath.

"Can I grab a ride home?" she asks. I tilt my head.

"Thought your dad said you were going out tonight?" I ask. She swallows and tucks a long strand of hair behind her ear.

"I guess I'm not really feelin' it," she says. "Is that cool?"

I nod.

"Of course," I say. Then, I walk around to the passenger side and open the door. She pauses for a moment and looks at me, and I realize this is the first time someone's done this for her.

She smiles and turns to me.

"You don't have to do that, ya know," she says.

"It's how my Grannie raised me," I tell her. She smiles again.

"I respect that. It's just that I...uh..."

"You...uh...what?" I ask.

"I can open my own door," she says sheepishly. I nod as a smile tugs on the corner of my lips. Most girls my age that I take in this truck fawn over this simple gesture. Like they've never had a damn door opened for them in their lives, let alone a male to actually acknowledge that they are a living, breathing human being.

"Ya know, Tess," I say, "I haven't known you long, but I'm beginning to think there's not a lot you *can't* do. It's just that you don't always *have* to."

She thinks about my response for a minute, then climbs in.

And that's the moment I swear to myself that, in my presence, Tess Connor would never open her own door. I roll the windows down a little bit and reach for the radio dial. My truck's not the newest, and I don't have any sort of fancy music set up. But what I do have is my New Edition greatest hits CD, and there's never a bad time to play that.

I turn it on and start pulling out of the lot when I feel her eyes on me.

"What?" I ask her.

"New Edition?" she asks. I raise an eyebrow.

"What do you know about New Edition?"

She smirks.

"Your chief has an eclectic musical taste," she tells me. "They're on all the time in our house."

"I knew I liked him," I say. "He has good taste."

She laughs.

"Easy, Bobby Brown," she says, holding a hand up. "They're *alright*."

I playfully hit the brakes.

"That's it. You don't disrespect New Edition in my truck. Out."

She rolls her eyes and leans back in the seat.

"Easy, Bobby Brown," she says again with a smile that warms me from the inside out.

twelve years ago
16 + 28 YEARS

CHAPTER FIVE

cade

"FUCK," I say as Chief puts the truck in park in front of the small farmhouse that's glowing in orange light. It's not a big house, but it's completely engulfed. Flames spill out of the windows and the front doorway. Dirk runs to hook up the hose as the rest of us jump out, running up to the lawn. A young woman covered in soot and ash looks at us with glazed eyes as she rocks her infant, a toddler clinging to her leg below.

"Ma'am," I say as we approach her, "is anyone else in the house?"

When she doesn't answer, Chief, Dirk, and the others run toward the house.

"Ma'am," I try again, "is anyone else in the house?" I recognize the look of shock in her eyes. We see it a lot. Like they realize that their whole lives are turning to ash in front of them, but in the moment, they're hypnotized by the flames.

"Just the dog," she says, her voice hoarse. I nod and charge toward the house, following the others.

"Guys, there's a dog inside!" I call out as I start to hose down the house. The roar of the flames is deafening, and I'm already sweating in my suit.

I hear them pass the message from person to person, everyone trying to lay eyes on the dog.

After a few minutes, we finally hear Jim from the other side of the house.

"Got him!" he says. "He's still breathing!"

I let out a sigh of relief as I continue to hose, when suddenly, we all hear the loud sound of wood cracking from behind the house.

"Fuck, Chief!" I hear Jim call, and my heart pounds in my chest. I drop my hose and run around to the back of the house to see that the entire deck has collapsed. And underneath it, lies my chief.

Dirk, Rich, and I are sitting in the ER waiting room a few hours later. We managed to free Chief just as the EMTs were arriving. We got him in the ambulance while the rest of the guys finished working on the fire. We got here as fast as we could. I look around for Tess, but she's nowhere to be found, and I wonder if she knows. Just as I'm about to ask, a nurse comes into the room and asks for Dirk.

I can't hear everything, but I make out "broken arm" and "stable" and I breathe a little easier. Dirk turns back to us.

"Looks like Chief has a broken arm and some scratches, but otherwise looks okay, somehow. They're taking a few more X-rays and running a few more tests, then we can see him." I nod.

"Did anyone let Tess know?" I ask.

Dirk nods.

"Mel called her. She went to pick her up from her friend's. She should be here soon."

Another sigh of relief. Poor girl is probably fucking terrified.

I fell right into line with the rest of the guys at the station when it came to Tess. Over the last year, I've become protective as hell of her. I watch her spend her free time in the station, studying, cleaning up, making the guys food and coffee. For a sixteen-year-old, she's very in tune with what people around her want and need. I just wonder if anyone is in tune with that for her.

"Hey, stranger," I hear from behind me, and I turn my head to see Lauren, a nurse I've become more than happy to run into whenever we stop by the hospital. I stand when I see her, wanting to melt when I see her in those damn scrubs, like a slow-motion scene from a dirty movie. For something created to protect people from the most gruesome, gross medical scenarios, she makes them look so damn good. I don't understand the power of scrubs, but I know I've fallen victim to them.

Her dark hair is pulled into a bun at the top of her head, and despite having worked for God knows how long tonight, she still smells fucking delicious. We've grown...close over the last few months. She's friends with some of the EMTs that hang at the station, and I've been foaming at the mouth to get her alone.

"Hey, you," I say, pulling her in by her waist and give her a hug.

"Heard you guys had a tough one tonight," she says when we come apart. "Is he okay?"

I nod.

"Couple of scratches and a broken arm, but he's gonna be fine. You know that man ain't going nowhere," I tell her with a smile. She smiles back.

"I hope you're not either," she says.

"Only if it's with you," I say. She smiles again and bites her lip. "Speaking of which, do you have plans this weekend? Some of us were gonna go get some drinks on Friday."

"I'm actually off on Friday," Lauren says with a smile, "so I'd love to." She pushes up against me, and I feel my dick stiffen. Just as I'm about to charm her even further, I feel a mini tornado blow past me through the waiting room doors as Tess makes her way through the aisles of chairs to the front desk.

"Hi, I'm Tess Connor," she says to the woman behind it. "I'm here to see my father." Dirk joins her at the front.

"Hey, sweetie," he says. "His nurse just came out to talk to us. He's gonna be fine. They're coming to take us back in just a minute."

I see her nod quickly and take in a breath, and I immediately feel this pull to her. I want her to know that she's okay. That *I'm* going to make sure she's okay.

Just then, the nurse appears at the doorway again and motions for Dirk and Tess to go back. Just before she turns to follow her, her eyes lock on mine from across the waiting room. I smile, but she doesn't return it. Her eyes float from me, to Lauren, then back to me, and I can feel the air in the room grow colder. She narrows her eyes on me before turning her back to all of us and heading back to her dad.

I turn back to Lauren.

"Great. It looks like they're letting us back to see him, so let me go check on him. I'll call you tomorrow so we can make a plan," I tell her. She smiles and nods, squeezing my hand as I walk by her. I jog a bit to catch up with the nurse, Dirk, and Tess, but I hold back once I do to keep my distance. When we get to the room, Tess is in front. Before she goes in, I watch her outside the door as she collects herself. She draws in a long breath and closes her eyes for a brief moment, and I fight the urge to reach out and touch her hand. She doesn't open them. She just stands there, breathing in slowly through her nose with her eyes closed and forcing the breath out with pursed lips.

Over the past year, I've come to find out that Tess, although she seems like she has it all together, is chronically early to everything, makes sure the guys are fed, and that the unmarried ones have taken their daily medicines, vitamins, etc. She's anal about everything because she doesn't want to miss anything. She seems overly organized, but it's because she's terrified of something going wrong. She has to be in control of every situation, otherwise, her anxiety controls her. She carries the weight of her father, and although she adores him, he has no idea what she holds for him.

"Hey," I say, just above a whisper. Slowly, she peels her eyes open and looks at me. "I'm right here."

Her eyes widen a bit, and she nods slowly. She clears her throat and walks into the room. Dirk and I are right behind her.

"Hey, kiddo," Chief Connor says. I didn't think it was possible that someone could look manly in a hospital gown, but Jack Connor does in the damn thing.

She doesn't say anything, just rushes to his side and wraps her arms around his neck as gently as possible. He rubs her back with his IV-less hand.

"We're okay, kiddo," he says. "We're okay."

She steps back, and I can see that her eyes are glassy, but she clears her throat again and swallows them back. Not a single tear falls down her cheek.

"You scared me, Connor," she says to her dad. "Do I gotta follow you everywhere?"

He laughs, his belly moving up and down under the gown. Jack Connor is a large man. He's about six-foot-two with big shoulders and a bit of a belly. He's not in the best shape, but I'm pretty confident he could still kick my ass and pretty much anyone that dared rival him. He's got strawberry-blond hair—what's left of it, anyway—that's tinged with white and gray, and a goatee to match. He's got tattoos on both arms and dresses in navy t-shirts and jeans every single day.

He's the best boss I've ever had, and for being the only Black kid on the job, I've never felt singled out a day since I got to Dalesville. I might be half-white, but that carries little weight when all people see is brown skin.

"Y'all didn't have to come down here," he says to Dirk and me, and Jim, who has now appeared at the door. "I'm all good."

Rich laughs.

"You didn't look 'all good' when that whole damn deck was on top of you," he says. But the room gets quiet quick when we all notice Tess's face. I take a step closer to her. I want her to feel my presence. But she moves away from me and closer to the door.

"I'm gonna go grab something from the vending machine. Have y'all eaten? Anyone need anything?"

We all shake our heads.

"We're good, kiddo," Chief says. "Hurry back."

She nods and scurries out of the room like a mouse, hands tucked into the pocket of her hoodie as she goes.

Chief looks at all of us.

"That girl is gonna have a heart attack before she's twenty," he says, shaking his head. "I worry about her worryin' so much."

"I'll check on her," I tell him, and he nods. I walk out of the room and turn down the hallway where I see her long auburn locks flying around the corner. She hits the button for the elevator just as I'm catching up to her.

"Hey, wait up," I say just as the doors slide open. She gets on but makes no motion to hold the doors. "Gee, thanks."

She doesn't say anything, just leans back against the elevator wall and looks up at the fluorescent lights.

She's tapping her foot so fast it's making the elevator shake.

"You good?" I ask. She bites her bottom lip as her eyes scan the top of the elevator.

"I don't like elevators," she says. "I normally take the stairs, but I couldn't find them. And I just want to get back to Dad."

I nod slowly.

"Well, ya know, part of my job is getting people out of these bad boys. So, you just happen to be with the right person, worst-case scenario."

I'm hoping for a smile, a loosening up of some sort. But nothing. Finally, the doors open again, and she walks out, leaving me in her dust. I follow behind her, down the hall to the cafeteria. She scans the refrigerators, then settles on a bottled iced tea. I smile when I see the one she takes.

"Unsweetened, huh?"

"Sugar ruins the natural tea flavor," she says. I reach around her and catch the door before it closes, grabbing one for myself.

"Agreed."

I snag her bottle and pay for both at the register before heading toward the doorway.

"You didn't have to do that," she says. After a beat, she adds, "But thank you."

Another Tess quality I've become familiar with: she's fiercely independent. If you didn't know her, you'd probably think she is way older than she actually is. She cooks dinner for herself and Chief every night—which, most days, means leftovers for us—works four days a week at the pizza place in town to save for her own car, and makes sure the dogs are fed and walked when Chief has late shifts.

She's a sixteen-year-old living out the life of a woman in her twenties or thirties. It didn't take long for me to see that she's filled the role of woman of the house. She cares for Jack like a wife or a mother would. And he does his best—Lord knows that girl is his heart and soul—but it's also easy to see that he's at a loss when it comes to his daughter. He needs her a hell of a lot more than she needs him.

Just as I'm about to ask why she's giving me the cold shoulder, Lauren rounds the corner with another one of her friends, hands tucked into her scrub pockets, looking as cute as ever.

"Y'all following me or something?" I ask, but just as she's about to respond, I hear Tess scoff as she breezes by us. She hits the button, and I realize she, again, has no intention of waiting for me.

"Who's your friend?" Lauren asks, nodding toward Tess waiting in the hall.

"That's the Chief's daughter," I say. "Told him I'd keep an eye on her, make sure she's okay."

"Aww," Lauren says, looking out after Tess. "Poor girl's probably had a rough night." Then, she turns back to me, putting her hand on the side of my arm. "You're a good man, Cade. See you Friday."

I watch for a brief moment as her perfect ass sways in those scrub bottoms. My drooling is only stopped by the dinging of the elevator as it comes. And when I turn around, the doors are closing as Tess leans up against the wall again. I run, but I'm not fast enough. I press the button repeatedly, like an idiot, until the next car comes, and I get in, then press the button to close the doors just as idiotically. I get off a split second after she does, and now I'm a little hot under the collar.

"What was that about?" I ask, trailing behind her yet again as we walk back down toward Chief's room.

"What was *what?*" she says, refusing to look at me.

"Tess," I say, but she doesn't stop. "*Tess!*" I say again, loud enough that it makes her freeze in her trail. She whips around, her hair flying off her shoulders and down her back as she stares up at me. I tower over her and probably weigh double what she does, but she looks anything but intimidated. And if I'm being honest, *I* might actually be a little nervous right now. I almost laugh. Me. All of me scared of this little thing in front of me.

"The reason you're here right now is downstairs in that cafeteria," she says. "So why don't you go ahead and go back down? We're good here." Then, she turns on her heel and walks down to Chief's room, pushing the door open and going inside.

I follow a few seconds behind and stand against the back wall. The doctor is in the room, and Tess is standing at full attention at Chief's bedside.

"Sorry, I was downstairs getting a drink. Do you mind repeating what you told him? I just want to make sure I hear everything," she says. My heart swells a little for her. So damn responsible.

The doctor smiles.

"The lady of the house?" he asks Chief. Chief nods and smiles.

"She's in charge," he says. Everyone in the room chuckles, except for me and her. Because she shouldn't be in charge. Not at sixteen.

"I was just telling your dad that everything came back pretty good," he says. "Looks like a clean break in the arm, so he'll need to see an orthopedist and get the cast off in a few weeks. Scratches and bruises are all superficial, so that's good, too. They should heal up real nice. Your dad's BP is a little high, which is to be expected after tonight's events, but we're going to keep him overnight to monitor him. If all is well in the morning, we will discharge him then."

I watch her swallow as she nods.

"Okay, thank you," she says. The doctor leaves, and Dirk says his goodbyes, too. She kisses his cheek, then turns back to Chief. "I'm going to stay here with you."

He shakes his head.

"No, you're not. You need to sleep in your own bed. And you know them dogs will be chomping at the bit for you to get home. You gotta get some sleep, baby," he says. I feel relieved. The thought of her sleeping in jeans on the uncomfortable excuse for a reclining chair here doesn't sit well with me.

"I can take her home, Chief," I pipe up.

Before she can protest, Chief nods.

"That would be great, Cade," he says.

"Dad, I don't want to leave—"

"You heard the doc, honey," he cuts her off. "I'm fine. They will be waking my ass up all night to check

46

on me. They have your number if anything is off. Go home. Sleep. You can take care of me tomorrow."

I grit my teeth.

Who takes care of her?

She leans over him and kisses his cheek, then rests her head on his for a moment before standing up.

"Love you," she says as she walks toward the door, past me, and out into the hallway.

"Love you, baby," he says. Then, he looks at me. "Don't leave till she's in the door?"

I nod. "And till I know it's locked, sir."

He smiles and nods, then closes his eyes and lies back against the pillow.

We get back in the elevator, but she doesn't say anything. And I can't tell if it's that she's still pissed at me or that she's worried about her dad. Or maybe a combination of both. But all I know is, I want to fix it. I *need* to.

We're quiet as we walk out of the hospital and across the parking lot. I unlock my gray pickup and open her door.

"Thanks," she mutters as she watches me close her door.

I get in on the other side and start her up.

"Have you eaten?" I ask. She shrugs.

"I'll have something when I get home," she says.

"When's the last time you ate?"

She shrugs again.

"Earlier."

"We're getting food," I tell her. She doesn't fight me. She just leans back in her seat and lets me drive. I turn on the best of New Edition, and I notice a smirk on her face, as much as she tries to hide it.

A few minutes later, we're pulling through the drive-thru with our burgers and fries, and I'm parking at the back of the lot so we can eat. Within two minutes, she's scarfing her food down, and it makes me happy to watch her. To know that, for at least right now, she doesn't have to make any decisions—not for herself or for anyone else.

"So," I say as I watch her pop her last fry into her mouth and take a sip of her soda, "you gonna tell me why you were givin' me the business tonight?"

She keeps sipping, but I see the faintest hint of a smile playing at the corner of her mouth.

"Are nurses your *type*?" she finally asks, then puts the straw in her mouth again. I laugh and take a sip of my own drink.

"My *type*? I don't have a *type*. Why do you ask?" I say, feigning a little bit of innocence.

She rolls her eyes.

"Yeah, okay," she says. I laugh again.

"Okay, what's up?"

She shakes her head.

"Nothing. I just thought you might be more concerned about your boss than about catching some tail at a hospital, of all places," she says. I throw my head back and laugh again. I can't help it.

"Did you say, 'catching some tail'?" I ask, and I see her smiling out of the corner of my eye. "Listen, little girl," I tell her, and I watch as she rolls her eyes. My tone grows a little more serious now. "I don't go home till everyone else does safely. Ever. And that includes you. Don't you worry about what my *type* is. Just know that I take care of my people, and you are one of my people now. Okay?"

She stops sipping and looks up at me, those green eyes glowing in the fluorescent lights of the parking lot. She nods slowly, like she's really taking in what I've just said to her.

"Okay."

"Okay," I say, still trying to figure her out. "Let's get you home."

CHAPTER SIX

tess

I'M ROLLING the ground beef into balls and humming "My Girl" as I glance up at the clock. Dad should be home in ten minutes, and I am *so* excited. Dad and I spend a lot of time together, if you include my drop-ins at the station and me joining him and the guys at Andy's every few weeks. But it's actually very rare that we just spend time together intentionally. Dad's still in a cast, and although he's been helping out at the station with administrative stuff, tonight, he's not working. He should be home from the store any minute, and we're supposed to have dinner and watch *Smokey and the Bandit.*

I fully realize that most sixteen-year-old girls don't revel at the idea of staying home on a Friday night and watching movies from the seventies with their dad. But I'm not most girls. Most sixteen-year-old girls I know have a mom *and* a dad. They have loads of friends and are obsessed with their phones and breaking the rules while remaining angelic in the eyes of their peers.

I have a small world. It revolves around my grades, my father, and my dogs. Maybe the guys at the station, too. There is something so special about their line of work to me. Maybe it's that when they run toward the fire, they are doing it together. They're never alone.

Like when my mom died, we were never alone.

When Dad got hurt last month, we were never alone. Some of the station wives started up a meal train. Mel has been over at least once a week to bring some groceries, and Cade stops in regularly on his way home to check in.

Just as Dad walks in the house, my phone vibrates on the counter next to me. I see Mina's name light up on my phone, along with a picture of her aggressively kissing my cheek—the photo I picked for her contact.

"Perfect timing," I tell Dad. "Can you answer that and put it on speaker?" I ask, holding my meat-covered hands in the air. He does and walks by me to hang his coat up on the hook that hangs in the corner of the room.

"Hey, Meanie," I say, "you're on speaker because I'm making dinner."

"Hey, Mr. Connor!" she calls.

"Hi, sweetie!" he yells back.

"What's up?" I ask her, putting the last of the balls on the plate in front of me.

"A few of us are going to Pete Schwartz's tonight for a little get-together in his barn," she says. "Will you come?"

Just as I'm about to decline, I see my dad from the

corner of the living room, walking toward me briskly and nodding his head yes like a crazy person.

I knit my eyebrows together.

"Uh, hold on, Mina," I say, "let me check with my dad."

I hit the mute button and look at him.

"Uh, listen, kiddo," he says, and I feel the familiar feeling of coming second seeping in. "Mel had offered to bring by dinner tonight. I told her you were cooking, and she asked if I wanted to, uh, watch a movie, or maybe just hang—well, anyway, you're welcome to join us, but, er, I thought maybe you would want to go. I'm happy to drive you..." he says, and I realize what's happening. My dad has a date tonight and is trying to give me a hint that he doesn't want me third-wheeling.

I look down at the meatballs on the plate. I was making his favorite recipe tonight: dunky balls. Rolled balls with this homemade gravy that my grandmother used to make him. I sigh as I look down at them, swallowing the lump in my throat.

I hit the mute button again.

"Hey, Meanie," I say. "Yeah, I'll come. Can you pick me up?"

"For *real?* Oh my God, this day has to go down in history. Fuck yes I'll pick you up!" she shouts. Then, there's a long pause. "Oops. Sorry, Mr. Connor." Dad laughs.

"I'm a firefighter, honey," he says. "Fuck is the most popular word in my vocabulary."

I hang up with her and wrap the plate with plastic wrap and stick it in the fridge.

"You okay with this?" he asks. I want to scream at him. And tell him I'm not okay. That I don't want to go freeze my ass off in a barn full of a bunch of other teenagers. I want to stay home and have our favorite dinner while we watch our favorite movie. I just want to *be*.

"'Course," I say. "Can't believe my dad wants to get rid of me to get some ass," I say with a smile to let him know we're all good. I don't like when he's upset.

"Watch it," he says with a chuckle. "Mel is...she's nice."

I smile. Mel *is* nice. She's the station manager and knows her shit. And she keeps those guys in line when I can't be there. She got divorced a few years back. She and my dad...they actually make sense.

In ten minutes, I'm back downstairs after throwing on a pair of jeans, a cami, and a sweater, and Mina is calling me to tell me she's here. I kiss my dad's cheek and tell him to change into his navy button-up before Mel gets there.

"Be safe, kiddo," he says. "Call me if anything gets out of hand."

I nod and fake salute.

"Yes, Chief," I say before walking out the front door.

I get in the passenger seat of Mina's light-blue Jetta, and she immediately starts to tell me that this is a "very small get-together" and that she's "hoping tonight's the night with Tate."

All I know is, if he doesn't make his move tonight, I'm gonna kick him in the ass for being so dense and for taking his sweet-ass time. She's a catch, and he's an idiot. A few minutes later, we're pulling up the Schwartz's mile-long gravel driveway. They run a dairy farm on the far side of town, and they have a big barn that they rent out as an event venue on the property. When they're not busy, Pete likes to use it for parties. Or at least, that's what I've been told. I've never actually been to one.

When we get out, I realize that it's, in fact, a *very* small get-together in that it's just me, Mina, Tate, and Pete. I glare at Mina as we walk up the driveway. This was a set-up. Pete and Tate are best friends, and this was a "bring one for my friend" kind of deal. And I'm the fucking friend.

"God dammit, Mina," I whisper as the guys walk out of the barn toward us. She smiles at me as she squeezes my hand and rests her head on my shoulder while we walk.

"I loveeee you," she whispers in a sweet little voice.

"I'm not doing shit with him," I growl back. She shrugs.

"I didn't say you would," she says. "In fact, I told him you probably wouldn't be interested. Guess Pete likes a challenge."

"Hey," Tate says with a smile as we reach them.

"Hey," Mina says back, giving her best model-esque smile and hair flip.

"We have some drinks in the barn," Pete says. "'Sup, Connor." He nods in my direction. I want to barf.

Imagine going to second base with some asshole who greets you with, "'Sup."

I nod back and follow them reluctantly into the barn. A breeze blows, and I realize quickly that the barn has no heat.

Fuck this, Mina.

I shiver and run my hands up and down my arms. I jump when I hear the sound of metal scraping against wood. Pete is dragging a big iron fire pit through the barn doors and plops it in the center.

My daughter-of-the-fire-chief senses are tingling.

"Uh, that's probably not the safest place for that, right?" I ask, glancing around at all the wood and decorative hay. We're basically sitting in a barn full of kindling. My father would have a heart attack.

They all look at me blankly, and I am appalled at their lack of fire safety.

"There's no ventilation, and everything in here is wood," I say. Pete and Tate look at each other and chuckle.

"Relax," Pete says. "Don't call Daddy over it. We do it all the time," he says.

And then I want to smack him in the face. I glare at Mina again, and my face is saying "you fucking owe me" as she swallows nervously.

"I'm gonna go get some more wood," Pete says before turning and walking out of the barn. I look at the measly excuse for a fire he's started and smile. That won't be a threatening blaze anytime soon.

"I'm gonna go inside the house and make some

drinks," Tate says. Then, he looks at Mina. "You wanna come?"

She smiles like an idiot, gushing over his every move.

"Yeah, sure," she says. She looks back at me. "Be right back!"

I roll my eyes. And then I realize, after a moment, that this is actually the best-case scenario. I'm standing alone, inside of a pretty picturesque barn, and I don't have to pretend to be interested in Pete "Small-Dick" Schwartz.

I look around the barn and take it all in. There's a big dance floor in the center of the room with wood posts everywhere. It looks like the sides of the barn lift up—I assume for when the weather is nice—and the bales of hay add to the whole rustic theme. Then, I see a ladder in the corner of the room, and I walk toward it. I climb up it and find a small loft with just one table and two chairs. On the table sits a place card that says *Congrats to the happy couple!* and I realize this must be some sort of holding area for the brides and grooms before they have to join the party. And I think about how ridiculous that is. Imagine a party that *you* threw, that *you* paid for, and needing a break from it. But still, I find myself sitting down at the table, looking across at the empty chair, wondering what it must feel like to sit up here with the person you've just dedicated yourself to, looking out at all the other people who make your life complete, and who this room might be filled with if it were my wedding.

But my little daydream comes to a halt when I hear

two words that start the beginning of what is about to become the worst night of my entire fucking life. I smell it first. The smell of smoke and gasoline.

Then, I hear him.

"Oh, *fuck!*" Pete yells, and I run to the edge of the loft and look down. And then I see it. The orange blaze. I watch as the flames crawl across the trail of gasoline that's spilled from the can Pete dropped on the barn floor. I watch as they jump out of the firepit that's fully engulfed. I watch as they scatter across the wood and stick to every piece of hay, to the curtains on the window.

And I can't believe I'm a fire chief's daughter, stuck in a fire.

"Pete! What did you *do?*" I cry. He looks up and sees me, his eyes wide.

"What the fuck are you doing up there?" he shouts back, his face like he's seen a ghost. And I realize it's because, in this moment, he's not just worried about burning down his parents' barn. He's worried about killing someone. About killing *me*. I see him make a move toward the ladder, but flames encircle it.

I'm trapped in a barn on fire.

"Pete!" I scream. "Help me!"

I hear a fading scream as I see Tate and Mina in the doorway.

"Oh my God, Tess!" she shouts hysterically.

"Call 911, and then call my dad," I tell her. Then, I turn around and begin to try and save my own life.

I cannot leave him.

I look up and down. The flames haven't quite

reached the loft yet, but the barn is filling with smoke, and I know time is not on my side. Behind me, there's a small window at the top corner of the barn. I'm not even sure if I can fit out of it, but right now, that's the only shot I have. I run back toward it but realize it's too tall for me to reach.

I'm a fire chief's daughter, and I'm about to die in a fire.

CHAPTER SEVEN

cade

I TURN the water on as hot as it will go and let the week wash off me. My muscles are sore from the yard-work I did at Grannie's this morning, and I need to loosen up before my date tonight.

With Chief off the job for the last few weeks, we've all been pulling extra shifts at the station to cover for him. He'd do it for us in a heartbeat, and every single one of us knows it. But especially me. I've been here for a little over a year now, and I have never felt this at home at any station before. Jack Connor is far and wide the best boss I've ever had. When I first started here last year, I was still pulling doubles—working day shifts at the station, sleeping for a few hours, then heading off to Dilly's to work the bar. I've been bartending off and on since I turned eighteen, trying to carry my weight at Grannie's. It wasn't much, but I've never had much, so I know how to live off of it.

Jack started giving me more shifts when I wanted them, and after six months, he got me a decent enough raise to where I could quit the bar and just work at the station full-time. One job, one living, and a little time to myself—well, and to tend to things at Grannie's. I rent a small farmhouse a few minutes away from hers, but I spend a lot of my time there. It's the house she raised us in while my dad worked three jobs. My sister, Brenna, and I spent every day at Grannie's while Dad worked. Our mom left when we were kids and came around when it suited. But for all intents and purposes, Grannie raised us while Dad footed the bills.

Brenna moved down to Virginia a few years back, and Dad passed on my twenty-first birthday. So, it's just me and Grannie now. And that woman is my whole world.

But tonight, my world revolves around a cute little nurse and her tight little ass.

I step out of the shower and dry off, put on my best "going out" shirt, a pair of jeans that still have some life left in them, and a dab of the aftershave my dad used to wear. Spicy cedar is sort of a Waters men staple.

I look around the house to make sure it's suitable for company. Ya know, just in *case* Lauren wants to accompany me back for a night cap. Just as I'm about to walk down to the car, I reach for my wallet on the front table. But it's not there.

Fuck. I remember I left it in my locker at the station. I lock the front door and jog down the steps to my car, get in, and fly off to the station so that I'm not late picking her up. I've got a night of wining and dining—among other things—planned.

I park out front of the station and hop out, leaving the keys in the ignition. I jog in the front door and pass Mel at the front desk.

"Hi, Mel," I call as I breeze by.

"Hi, honey," she calls back, barely looking up from the magazine she's reading. She stops only when the phone rings.

I open my locker, dig out my wallet, and jog back.

But as I'm jogging back by, I freeze when I hear Mel.

"Oh, Jesus, not Tess," she says, her face a ghostly pale. "I'm putting in the call right now. They'll be there as fast as possible."

She hangs up and starts ringing the alarm. She runs toward the back of the station where the guys are sitting and talking. I follow her, and as I do, I notice she's shaking.

"Mel," I call back, "what about Tess? Where is Tess?"

"Barn fire at the Schwartz farm," Mel mutters. "Tess is there, stuck in the barn." But before she even finishes, I'm out the door. I grab a fire blanket on my way out and jump back in the car. I know exactly where the Schwartzes live because their dumbass kid started a fire in a trashcan last year that jumped out in the middle of a hayfield. Fucking little pyro.

I'm flying as fast as my truck will carry me until I finally reach the gravel driveway of the farm. It took about three minutes to get here, but it felt like a fucking lifetime. I know the guys will be right behind me, but I have to get there. I have to get to Tess.

But when I pull up to the house, my heart fucking

stops in my chest because I see Chief's truck parked right outside of the barn door, driver's side still open. And he's nowhere to be seen. So I know where he is. He went in after her.

"Fuck!" I scream as I jump out of my own truck, carrying the blanket. The barn is nothing but a swirl of orange and black, and I start sweating the instant I get to what's left of the entrance. I wrap myself in the blanket and dip inside, three hysterical teenagers watching helplessly as I do.

"Tess!" I scream when I get inside. I look to my right and see Jack trying desperately to reach her as she dangles from a two-story loft. "Jesus, Chief!" I dart toward them, but just as I do, the loft collapses. She falls on top of him, flames on every side. I quickly observe the scene ahead of me, and as I do, my heart stops again.

It's that feeling you get when the flames outnumber the bodies fighting it.

Hopelessness.

Because someone is going to die tonight.

My eyes meet Chief's for a brief moment, and we both know who it's going to be.

He lies under a mass of singed wood, but with all the might he has left, he shoves her in my direction.

"Go!" he screams. He and I both know we have mere minutes before what's left of the barn goes crashing down. I catch her in my blanket and wrap her up as she screams and tries desperately to get free and back to him. I drag her across the burning floor and out the barn door. As soon as I put her down on the ground, she makes a move back toward the barn. I look at the two kids standing next to me.

"Hold her!" I tell them. "If she gets back in this barn, I'll kill you both myself."

I see the red lights and hear the sirens wailing up the drive, but I know we can't wait for the team to get here. Every second counts. I wrap myself back in the blanket and go back in, but the flames have taken over the only path to Jack. I suck in a deep breath of fresh air out the door, wrap my feet in the blanket, and jump across the flames to get to him. But he's lying flat on the floor, the sleeve of his shirt on fire.

Not tonight, Chief.

I lunge for him, not feeling the flames that lick my body as I do. I know when the adrenaline wears off, this will be a bitch. But I don't fucking care. I grab him under the arms and hoist him up so that he's across my shoulders. I don't bother wrapping us in the blanket anymore. I just hoist him up and run toward the entrance. The guys are here now, running with hoses in position. An ambulance pulls up behind, and I lay Chief down in the grass. He's not moving. Not one bit. I start compressions and try to drown out Tess's screams in the background. The EMTs reach me, and I jump out of the way as they put oxygen on him. I take in the scene around me, Tess's screams, the guys fighting the fire. Even Mel came, and she stands in the background, clutching her chest and staring at Chief on the ground. The Schwartzes are finally home, and Mrs. Schwartz is screaming and crying as her husband cradles her. Tess is still wriggling to get free, and as I turn to her, she finally does. She's quick, but not quick enough. I reach my arms around and snag her off the ground, her feet kicking as I lift her.

"Tess," I whisper, but I know she can't hear me. Tears streak through the soot on her cheeks, and with every one that falls, I die a little more inside. "Tess," I say again. Slowly, the kicking stops, and the screams turn into sobs. I drop to my knees with her still in my arms, and finally, she gives in. I turn us so that I block her view of her father on the ground, his chest being pressed so hard that his body is caving in.

She presses her face to my chest, and I hold her tighter, wrapping my arms around her, trying to shield her from everything around her. But I know I can't forever. And her world is lying over there in the grass. I look down at my own hands and notice they're covered in blood. I pull her back from me.

"Tess, you're hurt," I say, looking her up and down, trying to figure out where it's coming from. But she doesn't say anything. She just cries against me, and I let her.

Just then, I see the EMT stop doing compressions out of the corner of my eye.

"DOA," he says quietly to the other EMT, who is radioing in.

"This is Unit 14," he says. "We are about to be en route with a DOA. Smoke inhalation and suspected cardiac arrest. Yes. ETA is about twenty minutes."

The guys put their hoses down almost in unison, only a few standing flames still remaining. Slowly, they all turn to us.

Tess pulls away from me slowly, looking first at me, like she's trying to gauge if what she just heard was real or not. She yanks away from me and out of my arms, but this time, I let her go. She runs to him, collapsing on the ground. She lies on top of him, clutching onto his body.

"Dad," she says, "please don't do this. Please don't leave me. Please," she gasps. Her shoulders shake, her tiny body convulsing. We all stand quietly for a moment, and finally, I kneel down next to her. She turns to me, her green eyes bloodshot and swollen.

"I can't..." she manages to choke out between sobs. "I can't...br...I can't breathe," she says, and I realize she's hyperventilating.

"Hey, hey," I whisper, reaching out to hold her steady. "Hey, it's okay. I'm right here. You're okay. We're okay."

But she shakes her head, her chest heaving and a wheezing sound coming from her. I look up at the EMTs, who make their way to us. Just as they kneel down, she keels over in my arms.

"Tess," I say, shaking her gently. "Tess!"

"She'll come to in a moment," the EMT says calmly as he slides an oxygen mask over her face. "We should probably take her in, too. Make sure everything checks out with her."

"She's bleeding from somewhere," I tell them. They look her up and down and lift up her shirt, revealing a huge gash on her ribs.

"Yeah," the other EMT agrees. He looks at me. "We need to get her in. This will need stitches. Does she have anyone you can call? Anyone who will meet her at the hospital?"

"She has an aunt in Massachusetts," Mel chimes in, her voice quiet as she tries to muffle her own sobs. "I can find her number. I think we have it at the station."

The EMT nods.

"Is there anyone that can meet her at the hospital? She's a minor, I presume?"

"I'm going to ride with her," I say. "I won't leave till her aunt gets there."

He nods as he and the other EMT lift her onto the stretcher and wheel her into the ambulance.

"Another bus will be here in just a minute to take, uh, Chief Connor to the hospital. Someone there will officially pronounce him. I'm sorry for all of your losses."

I climb into the back of the ambulance and sit on the bench next to the stretcher. Just as we're about to close the doors, Tess wakes up. She yanks the mask off her face and throws it, thrashing like a madwoman and trying to get up.

"Shit," the EMT says. He moves back toward her, trying to calm her down. "Ma'am, ma'am. I need you to—ma'am," he says, but she won't stop. I move over to her and grab her arms.

"Hey, hey," I say to her, looking into her eyes until I feel her calm slightly. "I'm right here."

For a moment, she stills, her pupils shrinking back down to somewhat normal size. But then she begins moving around again, and I see the EMT reach behind him, grabbing something off a tray and walking toward her.

"I have to sedate her."

I pause for a moment, then nod slowly as I continue to hold onto her arms. He shoots her in the arm, and momentarily, she's in a daze again, lying back on the stretcher and closing her eyes. I hold her hand in mine for the entire ride to the hospital.

A few hours later, I'm sitting in an uncomfortable chair next to Tess's hospital bed, staring at her while she sleeps. All of her tests came back fine, but the doctor wants to keep her on oxygen through the night and monitor her. He said that the trauma of the fire and losing her father might be a bad combination.

He told me a few minutes ago that I could leave and come back in the morning.

"The sedative we gave her will keep her out for a few hours," he said, "if you want to go home and get some rest."

I look at the clock. Her dad's sister, Marie, should be here in about four hours. I turn back to her. I can't fathom leaving her. I told the other guys and Mel that I'd stay till her aunt gets here, and they all left with the promise of returning first thing in the morning. I excuse myself and pull out my phone in the hallway. I hate calling so late, but I dial anyway.

"Hello?" Grannie answers, her voice scratchy with sleep.

"Grannie," I say, trying to get my voice low and

calm so I don't alarm her—well, alarm her more than I already have by waking her up at two in the morning. "It's me. I'm okay."

"What's going on, Cadey?" she asks.

"Gran, it's Chief Connor," I say. I pause for a moment.

"What happened, baby?"

"He died tonight, Gran," I say, "and Tess…" I feel my voice crack. I don't cry, but there's something about this, all of this, that has my chest tight and my throat dry.

"What happened to my girl?" Gran asks, panic in her voice. She's come to love Tess over the last year. Tess regularly checks in on her, too, and always brings some sort of food. Grannie has also started teaching her how to crochet.

"She's okay," I say. "But she's been sedated. I'm here at the hospital with her. Her aunt is coming in from Massachusetts. A barn caught fire, and she got trapped."

As I tell Grannie what happened, I feel my chest cracking. The thought of something happening to this girl, here. She's one of my people. I don't let things happen to my people. Chief was one of my people, too. And I couldn't stop something from happening to him.

I look at Tess again.

"The doc told me I should go home and get some sleep," I tell her. "But I…I can't…"

"I think you know what you need to do, baby," she says. "Talk to your daddy. Leave them marks on the moon. And whatever you do, don't let that girl wake up alone."

I nod.

"I won't, Gran," I say. "I'll call you when she gets up."

"Okay, baby. I'll be here, prayin' and cookin'," she says. "I love you, Cadey."

"Love you, Grannie."

I sigh and stare up at the fluorescent lights that illuminate the hallway. I'm not a religious man, but I talk to the people I've lost. Especially my dad. We didn't have the best relationship when I was a kid, but as I got older, I came to understand why he did the things he did. He was just doing the best he could with the tools he had. He'd know just how to handle something like this. I make a mental note that whenever her aunt gets in, I'll have a good old heart-to-heart with my dad.

When I walk back in the room, I freeze in shock when I see her big green eyes staring at me. I almost laugh. Sedatives might be tough, but Tess is tougher. Her eyes are open, but it's like she doesn't see anything. They just float around the room.

"Hey, Boss," I say as I take the seat next to her bed. I reach for her hand again, but she flinches when I touch her. "Can you hear me, T?"

She doesn't say anything, but her eyes finally find mine again. She's looking around at her own body like she doesn't recognize it. Her hands are bandaged from burns, but the worst injury is a bad gash up her side that she got when she fell from the loft. The nurse said it was superficial, but she'll have a scar. I see her wince as she raises her arms, feeling it.

She doesn't say anything about it, or about her hands. She just looks up at me.

"He's dead, isn't he?" she finally asks. I sigh and take her hand, not letting her take it back.

"Tess, look at me," I start to say, but she shakes her head.

"He's dead, isn't he?" she asks again, her voice firm. I nod slowly. I watch as heavy tears spill out from her eyes and slide down her cheeks. I reach a thumb up to swipe them away. We sit in silence for a moment as she weeps silently. "I have no one," she whispers, and my heart breaks a little more. I stand up from the chair and reach my arms under her, sliding her over in the bed. The burns on my hands from pulling them out sting under the bandages, but I don't flinch. I don't fucking care about a few burns. I climb into the bed with her and wrap my arms around her.

"You will never be alone again, Tess Connor," I whisper. "You got all those guys at the station. You got your aunt. And most importantly, you got me. You are one of my people. And I am always gonna take care of you."

"He's gone," she cries into my chest, and I tighten my grip around her. "I didn't even say goodbye. He's just gone."

I think for a moment.

"Listen," I tell her. "When I was little, and I'd miss my granddad, Grannie would tell me to go leave my mark on the moon."

Her eyes are red and watering, but she stares back at me.

"What's that mean?"

"She used to say that all those marks you see on the moon are messages people leave for their loved ones who've passed on. And messages that they leave back. When I'd miss him or my dad, she'd tell me to leave a mark on the moon. So even still, I go outside, and I talk to the moon. It sounds silly, but it helps. So, when you miss Chief, you look up at the moon, and you leave your mark."

She nods slowly.

I know I'll be leaving my mark for Chief.

But as I look down at Tess, her tears staining my shirt, her body weak and helpless, I realize the moon isn't the only thing that will be marked by this girl.

CHAPTER EIGHT

tess

I'M AN ORPHAN.

The thought hasn't left my head in five months.

Aunt Marie has officially moved in. She's renting out her apartment in Rowe, the small town outside of Boston she loved so much. And that fucking kills me, because I know how badly she wanted to move north in the first place. She's all settled in the guest room—she says she can't bear to move into Dad's room and that it's too weird. I agree with her. I haven't opened the door once since he died.

She's great, really. Everyone has been great. My teachers have all been so patient. Most of them exempted me from my finals when everything happened, and a lot of them have given me extended due dates on projects I should have finished last semester. Normally, I get my shit done weeks in advance. But for the last few months, I've just been going through the motions of my life. Not really doing much, just being, watching everyone around me try and get back to normal, hoping to pull me along.

It's warm out now, which has been harder. It's easier to be invisible during the winter months. That's why they're my favorite. You can sit inside with a book and a blanket, and you don't need a reason.

Now, it's warm. Summer's on its way. People are wearing less clothes. Pools are opening. Parties are happening.

But I'm still in invisible mode.

Things have been weird with Mina. She wrote me an apology letter, and her mom continuously drops off meals and gift cards for Aunt Rie and me. I don't blame Mina. She was just being a teenage kid and just wanted her best friend to join her. I don't even blame Pete. I mean, it was his idiotic move to put the firepit in the barn. But I saw him do it. I still went in.

I knew better, but I didn't think. I did it anyway, and now the person who meant the most to me in the world is dead.

Mina invited me to a party with her in town tonight at the community pool. Dalesville holds it every year, sort of a summer kick-off sort of thing—potluck, music, too much alcohol, small-town drama. Usually, it's actually pretty entertaining, if you're watching it from afar. But right now, it feels like it's too much. Aunt Rie is going and really wants me to join her. I know she's worried, but I just can't fathom having to force a smile, tell acquaintances that I'm "hangin' in there," or pretend to care about anything else that's happening in their lives when I can't even effectively live my own.

She comes into my room as I'm lying on the bed, clutching onto a pillow and reading *To Kill a Mockingbird*. It's my favorite book of all time, and Dad's the one who got me hooked on it. He said he had never read another book assigned from school but that this one changed his life. He played Atticus in the school play and everything. It makes me feel closer to him. Like he's sitting here with me, reading over my shoulder.

"Hey," she says with a light knock on the door. "You gonna come tonight? I think it would be really good for you."

I roll over and face her, putting the book down on my bed.

"I don't think so, Aunt Rie. I will be fine here, though. You should go," I tell her, trying to sound convincing and knowing all the while that I am failing miserably.

The thing about depression is that you're drowning, and sometimes, everyone else sees it but you. But the other thing about it is that the only person who can pull you out of it...is also you. You have to save yourself from something you don't even know is killing you. And sometimes, all the people that love you can do is just wait and hope that you figure it out in enough time.

She sighs and pats my hand, then walks out of the room. I hear her a moment later, talking on the phone. She's trying to whisper, so I move to my door to eavesdrop.

"No, she says she doesn't want to go," she says. "I know. I know. I wish I could get her out of this house.

Her therapist says this is pretty standard with grief. Yeah. I know."

I knit my eyebrows together, trying to figure out who she might be talking to. We don't have much family left. Both of my dad's parents died when I was a kid. My mom's parents cut ties with my dad and me after she died—gems, those ones—so all we really have is each other. There are a few cousins on my dad's side that Aunt Rie keeps in touch with, but not regularly. I hear her again. "Oh, sure. If you want to give it a try, be my guest."

I hear her say goodbye, then I flop back on my bed, wondering who my next guest will be.

Twenty minutes later, there's a knock on our door. Aunt Rie opens it, and though I'm straining to hear, I can't make out the voice. I hear their footsteps below, then I hear them both walking up the steps.

"Tess," Aunt Rie calls on her way up, "you have a visitor."

I sit up in bed, tighten the rat's nest that sits on top of my head, and fold my arms over my dad's sweatshirt that I've basically been living in since he died.

But I'm a little shaken when Cade walks through the door behind her. I clear my throat and sit up straighter, trying not to look like the fucking disaster I have morphed into. But it's much too far gone.

"Should we start having your mail forwarded to this room?" he asks with that sly half-smile that I can't help but reciprocate. I bite my lip and shake my head. "What's up, Boss?"

I shrug.

"Same 'ol, same 'ol," I say. I hold my arms out. "Livin' my best life."

"Uh-huh," he says, looking around my room. "I can see that." He sits down on the bean bag chair that's in the corner, then looks up at us. "You know one of y'all is gonna have to help get me out of this, right?"

Aunt Rie holds her hands up.

"Sorry, I gotta go finish wrapping the food for tonight. Best of luck to you," she says with a wink, then heads downstairs.

He turns to me and leans back in the chair.

"What's up, Boss?" he asks again. "What's *really* up, I mean. Not the same B.S. you been feeding to Marie."

I swallow and look at him. There's something about Cade that makes it hard to hide anything. I guess when a person has seen you die inside, watched the life get sucked right out of you, held you while you fell completely apart, it's impossible to hide much else.

I sigh and hug my knees to my chest.

"Just don't feel like doing much," I say with a shrug. He nods slowly.

"I get that. So, what *do* you feel like doing?" he asks. I look up at him. No one's asked me that yet. Just made suggestion after suggestion of what I *should* do, or what I *could* do. Not asked what I *want* to do.

I sigh.

"I just want to make it through a day without being reminded that my dad died in front of me, trying to save my life."

He pushes his bottom lip out in thought, nodding slowly.

"Guess that's been pretty hard to do around here, huh?" he asks.

I nod.

It's like my father was the king of Dalesville, and his royal subjects are still grieving.

"What about a trip? What if you and Marie went somewhere?"

I scoff.

"I can't outrun my own skin," I mutter out loud before I realize I've done it. He cocks an eyebrow.

"What?"

I bite my lip.

"What does that mean?" he asks. I scoot to the edge of my bed slowly and reach for the hem of my oversized sweatshirt. I see him swallow, his eyes darting to the doorway, then back to me.

I pull it up slowly, watching as his eyes follow the long, jagged scar up my rib cage. His eyes finally meet mine.

"My own body is a reminder of the night he died... because of me. I literally wear it like a fucking badge. I can't outrun it."

He stands up from the beanbag and walks over toward me, pulling me up from the bed. Then, he puts a finger under my chin and lifts my face up to his.

"I'm right here," he whispers, and suddenly, my body feels weak.

I feel my lip start to tremble, and I don't even know exactly why. I don't know why those three words are setting off waves inside of me. It's like someone is finally giving me permission to grieve. Someone's

77

letting me do what I need to do to get the complete and utter anguish out of my body. I feel my eyes start to burn, but I don't bother holding them back. I let them fill my eyes until they spill over, and my whole body starts to shake.

He pulls my head to his chest and strokes the back of my hair.

"Is this what you've been wanting to do?" he asks. "Let it all out?" I nod. "Then, that's what we're gonna do, Boss," he whispers. And I do. I cry hard, loud, shoulder-shuddering sobs against him, much like the night my dad died. He just sits still, letting me expel it, absorbing it all into him like he's trying to catch it and hold it back from getting me again.

When I've finally calmed down, I hear my aunt appear in my doorway. She looks at him, then at me.

"Oh, sweetie," she whispers, her own lip starting to quiver. But I wipe my eyes and face, tucking my hair behind my ears as I sit up from Cade's chest.

"I'm okay, Aunt Rie," I assure her. "I just needed to, uh, get that out, I guess." She nods slowly.

"Hey, Rie, can I talk to you for a second?" Cade asks. She nods, then he looks down at me. "You good, Boss?"

I nod, a little embarrassed.

"Yeah, yeah," I say, "I'm good." He squeezes my hand and follows her out the room and down the stairs. I go into my bathroom and wash my face, dabbing at my swollen eyes with a cool washcloth. When they're bloodshot, like they are right now, my eyes look blue instead of green. My dad would always say, "Where'd my green-eyed girl go?"

I'd smile through my tears, wishing them away just so that he wouldn't be worried. Even if I wasn't ready to stop crying. Even if I was still torn apart inside. I had to be his green-eyed girl again.

I comb my hair out and go back into my room. I slide my dad's sweatshirt up over my head and grab a clean one from my closet, pulling it on. When I turn back around, Aunt Rie and Cade are in my doorway again.

"So," Aunt Rie says, "we're not going to the picnic tonight."

I look at her and cock my head.

"Uh, okay," I say. "Where are we going?"

She looks up at Cade with a smile and nods in my direction.

"Just put some shoes on and come get in the truck," he says. I narrow my eyes at both of them, but I don't say anything else. I slip my shoes on and lead them both downstairs. Cade opens the passenger door for Aunt Rie, then the back door for me, and we're off.

We drive past the pool that's packed with eighty percent of Dalesville's population, and I am increasingly glad we didn't go. I lean back against his seat, admiring his profile from my position. He has holes in his ears from earrings during his teenage years. When I asked him about them once, he said he was a little "wild" back then. He has a scar on his eyebrow that I like to look at it. There's something about Cade's imperfections that make him more enticing to me. Not just because he totally encapsulates the whole ruggedly handsome thing, but because it's a reminder to me that he's not perfect either and that he doesn't hold me to any sort of standard—especially the ones I hold for myself.

After about ten minutes, Cade has his blinker on, and I see he's pulling us into the Dalesville Tattoo Shop parking lot.

"What is going on here?" I ask as he puts the truck in park. They both turn around to me.

"Cade?" Aunt Rie says. He swallows and looks at me.

"I thought maybe we could come here and turn that scar into something that makes you happy. Something you don't wish you could run from," he says.

I swallow, feeling the lump in my throat again.

I look from him, back to her.

"I don't… I don't understand," I whisper.

"Cade is friends with the owner here," Aunt Rie says. "He called him, and his friend closed the studio for us tonight. You're sixteen, so you can get it with my permission. If you want it, you got it."

I look back at Cade.

"This was your idea?" I ask him.

He nods, our eyes locked on one another. I think for a moment. I hadn't ever thought much about getting a tattoo. But right now, knowing that Cade Waters did all this for me, knowing that I have some freedom to take my body and paint my own canvas over it, I've never been more sure about anything.

"Let's do it," I say. They both smile as I hop out,

and they follow me into the studio. When we get inside, a short man with shaggy blond hair, thick-rimmed glasses, and a nose ring greets us. He doesn't look like someone that most people would think Cade would be friends with. But that's the thing about Cade. I've never known him to fit into any box. He is who he is. Unapologetically. And for no one else.

"Cade Waters," the man says, clasping hands with him and pulling him in for a hug. Cade towers over him, wrapping him up in his big arms.

"Hey, Thad," he says, clapping him on the back. "How you been, man?"

Aunt Rie and I stand behind as they greet each other. Then, Thad turns to me.

"This is your girl?" he asks. I feel Cade reach an arm around me, pushing me forward, and for a moment, my stomach flips.

"This is her," he says, and there's something about those words, something about him saying them *about* me, that has me feeling out of sorts. For the quickest moment, our eyes lock again. I clear my throat and look back at Thad. He shakes my hand.

"I'm so sorry about your loss," he says, and I nod and thank him. "Cade here tells me you want to get a cover-up done."

I nod.

"Do you mind if I take a look?" he asks. I nod sheepishly, then raise my shirt slowly. He pulls me toward a bright lamp that stands in the corner of the studio so he can examine the scar. He runs a finger over it, then looks back up at me.

"We can definitely do something with this," he says. "Did you have anything in mind?"

I pause for a second, then I look up at Cade. I only found out I was getting this ten minutes ago. But somehow, right now, I know exactly what I want.

I turn back to Thad.

"Yeah," I tell him. "I know exactly what I want."

ten years ago

18 + 30 YEARS

CHAPTER NINE

tess

I FIDDLE with the tassel on my graduation cap as Andy's roars around me. They closed down the place so that Aunt Marie could throw my graduation party here. She was a little concerned when only four people from school showed up and was even more confused when the majority of my high school graduation party attendees were forty-plus-year-old firemen. But I wasn't confused. I was happy.

These are my people.

These were *his* people.

And some of them are as close as I can get to being with my dad.

Their wives and families came earlier, but by now, most of them have left. Mel is chatting in the corner with Aunt Marie while Rose brings more beer. As she sets down the pitcher, she slides something onto the table in front of me. When she lifts her hand, I can see it's a card. I look up at her and see that her eyes are glassy.

"Just wanted to get you a little somethin' to get ya started," she says. "It ain't much, but it's somethin'." She pauses for a moment, like she's collecting her thoughts. "You've been through so much, sweetie, and you're still just as wonderful as ever. We're all gonna miss you around here."

I stand before the tears spill over and wrap my arms around her. She's been a familiar and welcomed face for most of my life, and I truly will miss her. I'll miss a lot next year when I'm down at Salisbury. I start in two months, and the plan is to work my ass off and apply for the nursing program there.

If Dad were still here, I know I would have chosen a closer school, another program that would have let me stay home. He'd need me. But since he died, so much that once filled me with that feeling of being home just doesn't anymore, and I find myself feeling like a stranger in my own life.

Just as I let my arms down, the bell above the door chimes, and the guys raise their glasses in unison. That's when I lay eyes on him, on one of the constants, one of the people that still reminds me that I *am* me.

It's been three years since I met Cade, but I know him so much better than so many other people who I've known so much longer. It's because he asks. He wants to know. He makes sure school is going well. He gets why I don't have a lot of friends, but it doesn't concern him.

He knows about the poems I write, although he's never read them—no one has—and I've never once feared that that sacred secret would get out. Some nights, when I still meet the guys here at Andy's, he knows that when I'm quiet, it's time for us to go outside and leave our marks.

I smile when I see him, when I watch the joy he brings to the room. He walks in and starts his hellos, high-fiving, handshaking, squeezing shoulders. He kisses Mel's cheek, then hugs Aunt Marie, then finally stops at me. His smile is big and devious, and I know what's about to happen. I roll my eyes playfully and put my hands up.

"Oh, hell no," I say, but I know it's too late. He dives into me, pulling me up from the booth and throwing me over his shoulders, spinning me around while the guys cheer.

"Our little baby's all grown up, fellas!" he says, and they all laugh and put their beers in the air. He sets me back down and pulls me in for a real hug. "I'm so proud of you, Boss," he whispers, and the tone in the air shifts a little. I look up at him, and he narrows his eyes on mine. He takes the seat next to me, asking all kinds of questions. Have I started dorm shopping yet? When do I find out about my roommate? How long do I have? And I happily tell him every little detail, knowing all the while that he is stashing them away, never to be forgotten. He doesn't seem to forget anything about me.

We talk for a while, and for a bit, I think this is the happiest I've been since I lost Dad. Right here, with my eyes on my people, making sure they are all laughing and happy and safe. Comfortable being quiet and invisible, but not missing a single thing. And then I hear

Cade's laughter roar next to me, and it makes it that much more euphoric.

But just as I turn to him, I see his eyes narrow in on something—or someone—across the bar. And there at the door is none other than Lauren Felix, the oh-so-perfect nurse that won't seem to disappear from my life. She was there the night my dad broke his arm—with Cade in tow. She was there the morning after my dad died when they discharged me, overly responsive to me, disgustingly sweet, and really fucking good at her job. Although I could have done without her calling me "girlie" every couple of minutes, I have to admit, she made my urge to become a nurse that much stronger. But I also could have done without watching Cade drool over her. I know they go back, but I don't care. He's supposed to be a part of *our* club. *Our* family.

Before I can say anything, I feel him stand up from the table. He reaches a hand down to my shoulder.

"I'll be back," he says, but his eyes never leave her. I watch as he walks toward her, grabbing her in his arms and giving her one of those long, drawn-out hugs. In a moment's time, Mel and Aunt Marie are back at my table, still chatting away. The rest of the guys are still laughing and talking, beer spilling on the table, pizzas sitting half-eaten in front of them. Rose brings me another root beer, but I'm not thirsty. I pretend to listen in on their conversations, but every few seconds, my eyes jump toward the bar area. I haven't seen Cade in a few minutes, and it's driving me nuts. I wish I knew why.

Finally, the guys start paying their tabs and boxing

up their leftovers. Aunt Marie asks for our tab, but Jim puts up his hand.

"No way," he says. "This one's for our girl."

I thank him and the rest of the guys and tell Aunt Marie I'm going to the bathroom before we leave. I'm hoping to get at least one glimpse of him before I go, to see what he's doing. As I round the wall toward the bar where the bathrooms are, I still don't see him. And then I feel panic set in.

Did he take her home? Did he leave without saying goodbye?

I sigh as I get to the bathroom, but just before I do, I catch a glimpse of something moving through the crack of the door of the closet. I take a step closer so that my eye is at the crack of the door, and I freeze. I hear them first. I hear the gasps.

I hear Lauren whimpering his name. I hear the labored breaths.

And then I hear Cade growl, and it sets off a visceral fire inside of me. I hate that he's growling right now because he's fucking someone else.

But I clutch my stomach because the sound of him feeling pleasure makes it flip.

I see him for a moment, hoisting her into the air in the dark closet.

"Take it, girl," I hear him growl, and I step back, pressing my back to the wall. I rush into the bathroom and lock the door behind me.

I walk to the mirror and stare at myself, my chest heaving with heavy, pained breaths.

I'm swirling with so many feelings right now that I can't even think straight.

I'm *mad.* I'm so fucking mad at him right now.

I'm mad that he ditched me at my own graduation party.

But as I stare at myself in the mirror and draw in a long, slow breath, I realize that it's not so much anger I'm feeling.

It's devastation.

Because Cade Waters is having sex with someone. He's having sex with someone else who has probably had sex before. He's doing things to her just a few feet away from me. And that woman will have him in ways I never can.

I want Cade Waters, and I will never have him.

I throw some water in my face and unlock the door. Just as I'm getting myself together, Cade is stepping out of the closet. He freezes when he sees me, and I hold his gaze for a minute. Then, I storm past him and back to the table.

"Aunt Marie, I'm not feeling great," I tell her. "I think I wanna head home."

She looks at me with a furrowed brow. She and Mel were deep in conversation, and I can tell she doesn't want to leave. But she reaches for her purse and throws her phone inside.

"Oh, no," she says. "I'm sorry, honey. Let's get you home."

"I'll take her," I hear a booming voice say behind me. "I'm about to head out myself. I'll take her on my way home so you ladies can finish your evening."

God dammit.

"Oh, thank you, Cade," Aunt Marie says. She looks back at me. "Is that okay, honey?"

Fuck you, Waters.

I want to say no. I want to leave with her.

But she's happy, having a good time. She's given up so much for me, and I remind myself of that every single day.

I turn to him slowly.

"Sure."

I turn and head for the door.

"See you at home, Aunt Rie," I call over my shoulder.

"Okay, honey."

I feel Cade on my heels as I lead him to his truck. I walk to the passenger side door, and per usual, he follows me, pressing the unlock button on his key fob and pulling it open for me.

"Thanks," I mutter as I climb in and let him shut the door. I immediately go into fight mode—I've got my legs tucked under me, my body positioned away from him, and my eyes out the window.

He gets in and starts the truck up, blasting the air and turning the vents in my direction.

He doesn't say much to start, and I think it's because there's not a whole lot to say.

He pulls out onto Main Street, and we drive quietly through the streets of Dalesville until he turns onto Clark Drive. I know we still have two-point-three miles to go before he reaches my house, but it feels like our time together is drawing to a close.

But I won't say a word. Not until he does. Mostly because I have no idea what to say.

The drive is cold and quiet, and a few minutes later, he pulls into my driveway and puts the truck in park. I reach to unbuckle myself, but to my surprise, he puts his hand on top of mine.

"We gonna talk about tonight?" he asks. I suck in a breath and look out the windshield.

"What's there to talk about?" I ask, my eyes dropping to my hands.

"Don't do that, Tess," he says. I don't say anything, and I feel him nudge me. "Hey. I'm right here. Let's talk."

I close my eyes for a moment, the butterflies in my stomach churning at turbo speed. I slowly turn to him and open them, and as intensely as I feel toward him, everything melts away the second my eyes lock on his. I hate that.

"Okay," I say. "Talk."

He draws in a breath.

"Did you...see..."

"Did I see you fucking Nurse Lauren in the utility closet at Andy's?" I blurt out. His eyes
are wide. "Yes. Yes, I did." He sits back in his seat and scratches his brow.

"Tess, there's...there's not a lot for me to say except that I'm sorry," he says. "Lauren and I have history, and we hadn't seen each other in a while, and..." His voice trails off, probably because he can smell the bullshit in his own words as much as I can. "There's no excuse. I shouldn't have ditched like that. Tonight was about you."

I look down at my hands again as I fiddle with a stray thread coming out from the seat. I grit my teeth because I don't know how to tell him that it wasn't even that he ditched.

It was so much more than that.

So instead, I lie.

"It's fine," I say. "You're a grown man. You do you. You don't owe me anything."

He narrows his eyes on me, and I can feel the heat coming off of him.

"Hey," he says, and I let my eyes meet his. "I know I don't *owe* you anything. Life isn't about who we *owe*, Tess. It's about the people who are important to us, and you're important to me. I didn't show that tonight, and I'm sorry. I let you down, and it won't happen again. I am always gonna take care of you."

There's another long pause while I contemplate telling him that I was most upset because *I* wanted to be the girl in the closet. And how I will most definitely be thinking about him telling me to "take it" while I'm in the shower tonight.

"I got you something," he says. He reaches across my lap and opens the glove box. He pulls out a small square box and hands it to me. "Happy graduation," he says. I look up at him, then down at the box in my hands.

"You didn't have to—" I start to say, but I stop when he gives me a look.

"Open the damn box, Boss," he says. When he calls

me *Boss*, he's messing around. He calls me by my first name less, but it's always when the situation is more serious. I asked him once why he switched it up sometimes, and he said it was because he needed to get my attention.

I laugh and pull the top off the box. I lift the white tissue paper that's folded so neatly inside and see a bracelet. It's got silver beads with a pattern of purple and blue every few beads. It's beautiful.

"Purple and blue," I say quietly, with a smile.

"Purple and blue," he says. "My favorite and yours." I look back at the bracelet and pull it out of the box, sliding it over my hand. It's a little big on my skinny wrist, but I love it. "They spin," he says, pointing to it. I lift an eyebrow. "The beads. They're good for, uh, people who feel anxious. That's what it said online, anyway. So now you don't have to twist your hair into knots when I'm not there to stop you." We both smile, but my heart feels so full of emotion. He's the only person in my life who has seen what I perceive to be the ugliest part of me, yet, he seems to embrace them all the way. He doesn't run from them. Even if he doesn't understand them, he doesn't run.

"Thank you, Cade," I whisper. I feel my voice cracking a bit. No one's ever really gotten me like he has. He nods slowly, his eyes dropping from mine. "There also may or may not be a tracking device in that thing so I can keep tabs on you while you're at school."

I shoot him a look, and we both laugh.

Always the protector.

His eyes drop to the bracelet on my wrist.

"I'm gonna miss you around here, Tess," he says. I swallow. My heart is pounding in my chest. I want to crawl across the seat onto his lap. I want to inhale him. I want to tell him how much I'm going to miss him and how he is the only reason I don't want to leave Dalesville. I want to tell him how much he means to me and how I don't know what life looks like without him in it. But then he goes on. "But I'm so excited for you, girl. You're about to have some of the best years of your life, and you don't even know it. I'm so proud of you."

I force a smile.

He's *excited* that I'm going more than two hours away. He thinks I'm going to have the best years of my life, and he won't even be there.

And that's the moment I know I can't tell Cade Waters that I think I'm in love with him. Because Cade Waters has known me since I was fifteen years old. Cade Waters is "proud" of me growing up and going away. Cade Waters was having sex with someone else a half-hour ago.

Cade Waters isn't in love with me.

CHAPTER TEN

cade

MY PHONE GLOWS in my cupholder as I park my truck in my driveway a few minutes later.

It's Lauren.

Just before we snuck out of the closet to make what ended up being a less-than-stealth exit, I had told her I'd call her when I got home. Before I saw Tess's face, I had every intention of calling Lauren. I had every intention of starting things back up with her. We have history. We're both in tough lines of duty. We're friends with the same EMTs. And my line of work has landed me in the hospital a time or two.

She's a good person. She really is. She's smart, and sweet, and has the most bubbly personality. She's so good with her patients, and she's tough when she needs to be.

Plus, she's fucking hot.

But since my eyes caught Tess's earlier tonight, something has shifted. There was something in her expression that made me feel guilty for being with

Lauren. And it's not just that it was in a public place during what was supposed to be her graduation party. I already feel like the biggest ass in the world because of that.

It is something else. And I can't put my finger on it.

I reach up into my mirror and fold it down, pulling out the two photos I keep up there.

One is of Grannie and me. Grantstown had just won states, and she was the only one who came to watch me. I'm not smiling huge in the photo, but that's just because my teeth are a little crooked, and I hate my own smile. I was elated that day. My team had won, I had a few badass plays, and I had someone cheering for me.

The other photo is of the Chief, me, and Tess at a potluck dinner at the station a few years back. She's between us, with her arms around both of our necks. She had made chili that night, and we emptied the pot.

I keep it because I love her smile in it. It lights up her whole face, her eyes squinty, her cheeks round and stretched around it. I move my thumb to the picture, and before I realize what I'm doing, I'm using it to cover Chief's face so it's just me and her.

And the smile on my face is as big as hers.

I grab my phone in my cupholder, but I don't open the text from Lauren. Instead, I start a new one.

I snap a picture of the photo of us and send it to her.

I'll miss this. Go off into the world, and find something that makes you smile as big as this, I send.

After a brief second, she texts back.

Guess I need to take all you guys with me, then.

I smile as I look down at her words.

I lean back in my seat, pressing my head into the headrest.

I let out a breath as I realize I'd follow that girl anywhere.

"I'll see y'all in a few days," I call back into the station as I throw my boots over my shoulder and head out the door.

"See ya, Waters," Jim calls back.

"Bye, sweetie," Mel says.

I just worked a double, and I'm fucking spent. I want a pizza, I want a beer, and I want to sit on my couch and watch reruns of *Martin.* I get in my truck and drive a few blocks down Main Street to Andy's, the pizza place where Tess works.

Well, *worked* at.

I'm not the biggest pizza guy, but over the last few years, I've found comfort in it. Or maybe it's just that, after a long day, knowing she'd be there with a smile and that cute little black apron on was my reward.

I'll miss that.

But I'll still come because it will remind me of her.

When I walk up to the front counter, I stop in my tracks when I see her, back to me, with a tray over her shoulder, setting it down on a table.

I can't help but smile. I thought last night would be our last run-in before she left.

I look at the girl at the front counter as I hand her my debit card.

"Thought Tess was leaving for school," I say.

"Oh, yeah, she leaves tomorrow," she says. "She wanted to get one last shift in. Hoping for some good tips tonight."

I smile.

"Do me a favor," I say, signing my receipt, and pulling a one hundred dollar bill out of my wallet. "Make sure she gets this?"

The girl's eyes get wide, and she nods slowly. But before she takes it, I hear the growl of a man who's yelling, and my spine goes straight when I realize he's yelling at Tess.

"How fuckin' hard is it to get a goddamn order right?" he grumbles, his voice booming through the restaurant, making everyone else turn in their direction. Tess swallows, and I see her mumble something, trying to calm him down. "No, no," he screams. "This is just fucking ridiculous. We've been here a whole goddamn hour, it's taken forever for the food to get here, and now it's fucking wrong. And *you*—" he says as he pushes to his feet. He towers over her, but that's okay, because now, I'm between them, chest to chest, looking down at him.

"You have one goddam minute to get your shit and get the fuck out of this restaurant," I say to him sternly but quietly. I move so that Tess is completely eclipsed by me.

"You gonna make me?" the old man says, and I'm actually impressed by his courage. I lean down to him.

"That's exactly what the fuck I'm gonna do," I whisper. "So, if you don't wanna be swept up in front of a restaurant full of people and what appears to be your whole family, I suggest you leave on your own. Right now."

"Honey, come on," his poor wife pleads, but he just stares up at me, his buggy eyes narrowed.

He turns and grabs his coat off the back of the chair, and I think it might be a done deal. Till he walks past me.

"You fuckin' people," he grumbles under his breath. "Think you can come into *our* town and make it all…all fuckin' *ghetto.*"

I sigh and close my eyes, trying not to see red. He's an old man. He's out of shape. I'd quite literally kill him if I laid hands on him.

But frankly, right now, that's not sounding like such a bad idea. I clench my fists at my sides, my shoulders heaving with heavy breaths. Then, I feel her palms on my face, and I unclench my jaw, my fingers loosening as she speaks.

"Hey," she whispers. "Look at me."

I open my eyes slowly. I know we're standing in a restaurant full of people, but I don't care. Not one bit. All I hear is Tess's voice, bringing me back down. I'm lost in her. The brown specks in the green. And slowly, my lungs fill with air.

"Stay with me," she says, her thumbs stroking my cheeks. I nod slowly when I've gotten myself together. She cocks her head. "You good?"

I nod, and she smiles.

"Good. Now, excuse me," she says. She spins on her heel and takes her apron off, laying it on the front counter, and she storms out the door.

Oh, fuck.

I fly out after her, but she's too quick. She already caught up with the bearded bigot, and she's screaming in his face—all one-hundred-some pounds of her.

Fuck. If he touches her, I might have to kill him tonight.

"He is not 'you people,'" I hear her scream at him. "He's the best man I know and exposes men like you, who scream at women and berate people in public, for being the human scum you truly are. You can go fuck yourself, you backwards hillbilly piece of—"

"Tess," I say, taking her by the wrist and yanking her back, putting more space between them. But secretly, I want to smile. I thought I was the one who would kill for her. But I'm pretty sure, right now, the score is even. Because even I'm a little afraid of her in this moment.

The man looks down at her, then up to me.

"Humph," is all he says before he climbs up in his lifted pickup, closes the door, and peels out, leaving his wife and daughter standing on the curb.

Class act.

When he's out of sight, I turn and look down at her. She swallows.

I smile.

"What?" she says.

"Nothing, She-Hulk," I say, nudging her playfully.

She takes in another breath, then starts laughing. Then, she shrugs.

"I take care of my people," she says. "And you are one of my people."

I pull back for a moment, the smiles running away from both of our faces.

Yeah, I would follow this girl anywhere.

nine years ago

19 + 31 YEARS

CHAPTER ELEVEN

cade

IT'S BEEN months since I've been to Dilly's.

Shifts at the station have started to feel longer. It's winter in Dalesville, so things have been quieter. No roaring from the high school football field on Fridays, and we've had less calls lately.

Normally, I'd spend my free time fixing up the yard, but it's winter. I'd check in on Grannie, but she's not doing much these days. And I'd stop in for a visit at the Connor household…

But Chief isn't there. And neither is she.

I've checked in with her a few times. She called me every week to check in when she first got to Salisbury last year. But slowly, those calls came every other week. Then, once a month. Then, I stopped hearing from her. I still send her a picture of the guys occasionally when we head to Andy's. We video-call her when we're all together. I send her voice messages when her favorite songs play on the radio.

There's that one by Dave Matthews Band that she obsessed over. I pretended to get sick of it, but really, I loved listening to her belt that one out.

But now, things are just quiet. Still. Like, when Tess went away, the world slowed down a little bit. She came to Andy's once over her summer break last year. And that was the last I saw her.

Lauren and I started officially seeing each other around the beginning of fall this year, after years of hitting it but never quitting it. She's smart, driven, and hot as hell. We have a good time together, but there's a lot I've never said to her. A lot of things about me she doesn't know. But there are so many layers to me that sometimes I feel like it's easier to just keep it mellow, let people hear and see the parts of me they want to hear and leave it at that. I've been battling with my own shit for years. No need to stop now.

She's supposed to be meeting me once she gets off from the hospital, and so are some of the old crew that I used to work with here. Tonight will be a good night.

As soon as I walk in, I'm greeted from every side—some people who are coming back for a visit, some people who still work here at Dilly's and will probably never leave. I pull up a chair next to Darren and Mitch, two guys I used to work the bar with back in the day, and I have a beer in my hand before my ass is in the seat.

About twenty minutes later, Lauren walks in, looking as jaw-dropping as ever despite the fact that she was just nursing for twelve hours. Her tight little jeans do wonders for that ass, and I can feel the guys all stare at her as she walks toward me, planting a kiss right on my lips.

"I'm gonna run to the ladies' room," she says before she sits down. "Then I'll be back to meet everyone!"

They all nod, and I wink at her, then turn back.

Darren shakes his head.

"What?" I ask playfully.

"Shit," he says, "I will never understand it. You have never had a shortage of pussy in your life, have you?"

I shrug and take a sip of my beer.

"I have no clue what you're talking about," I say, and Mitch slaps my back with a hearty laugh.

"I mean, I guess you're not too bad on the eyes," he says as he takes a swig. I smile as I look up at the big TV that hangs above the bar. The truth is, I don't really think I'm the best looking. I take care of myself, I dress nice, and I *always* smell good. Grannie taught me that. But I think what it really is with girls is that I'm not afraid of them. I gravitate toward them. I listen when they speak.

I can't help it if that gets me into their pants now and then. But I'm not really a hit-it-and-quit-it kind of guy. I don't like jumping around. I like consistency. I don't let a lot of people into my life, so I can only handle so much.

She comes back out, and I introduce her to the old crew, and she's a hit almost instantly. They are doing their best not to drool over her as they pretend to be interested in how the hospital is or where she grew up. I look around the room as they chat, and I freeze when my eyes lock in on the girl who just walked into the bar. And as soon as I see her, the rest of the guys do, too.

"Damn," Darren whispers under his breath.

"Isn't that—" Lauren starts to say. I just nod. "Wow. She's really grown up."

"Damn right, she has," Darren mutters, and I shoot him a look.

"Stand down," I growl.

It's *her*.

Tess Fucking Connor.

And she's chumming it up with the bouncer who's blocking her path. He's a big dude, tall and thick, but I know, sure as I sit here, that I could take him if I had to. But it's not him that has me locked and loaded.

Even from farther away, she seems a little taller. A few girls I don't recognize walked in before her, flashed their IDs, and are already making their way into the entrance of the bar. But Tess is still at the door, batting long eyelashes and smiling up at the brute in front of her. He's smiling back, and suddenly, I feel my spine straighten. I stand up and excuse myself, walking toward the door. As I get closer, I feel a jolt when I get a glimpse of her whole body. She has hips I don't recognize, her lips round and full, with perky, perfect breasts that bounce as she laughs at him. I wonder how so much could have changed in just a few short months.

I see him lean down as I get closer, whispering something in her ear. She smiles back at him and nods, and I see her place a playful hand on his chest.

My insides are on fire as I get closer.

"Boss," I say as I approach them. Her friends have dispersed into the bar now, obviously not interested in waiting to see her fate. But she's not concerned, because the bouncer now has his hand on her lower back, dangerously close to her ass.

Her eyes get wide as she lays them on me.

"Cade," she says in almost a whisper, like her breath ran away from her. She stands a little straighter, but Blockhead doesn't move an inch.

"What are you doing here?" I ask her.

"I'm, uh…I'm home for winter break," she says.

"No, I mean *here,*" I say. I realize it's not exactly the reunion I was hoping for when I saw her next, but right now, my concern is getting her as far away from this bar—and the ogre guarding its doors—as possible. Niceties can come later.

She glares at me but doesn't answer. I know what she's doing here. She's trying to get into a bar underage.

I don't know exactly why I do it. I could turn back and pretend I don't know how old she is. I could let her have fun. But letting her have fun might mean letting *him* have fun with her.

"Hey, man," I say, "she's nineteen." Her eyes are even wider now, her chest moving up and down with fast, uneasy breaths. He looks at me, then looks down at her. His hand slides down her back so that he's cupping her ass, and he looks back at me.

"Sounds legal to me," he says. My jaw ticks as I grind my teeth together.

"Dude, she can't come in here," I say, stepping closer to him. "That's a fake." I point to the flimsy fake ID she handed him. But he pushes up from the wall, stepping near me so we're chest to chest.

Oh, man. You really don't want to do this.

"I'm pretty sure I'm the one who makes that decision," he says. "And she's looking pretty twenty-one to me tonight."

He lifts his hand up and reaches back for her, but before he puts his hand on her again, my hand wraps around his wrist.

"You don't want to do that again," I growl but in a hushed tone. I'm giving him a moment to reconsider. I'm too big of a guy—and too *Black* of a guy—to be angry in public unless it's for a good reason. But Tess… she's all the reason I need.

Instead of putting his hand on her, he steps toward me again, bumping me with his chest.

"Oh, I really think I do. And I think you need to get the fuck out of here before I kick your ass," he says. He steps back toward her.

"Hey, baby," he says to her, but before he can tell her to go in, I'm grabbing his arm again and twisting him up like a fucking pretzel. He wriggles loose and punches me square in the jaw. That's all I need. I lunge for him, clocking him on the side of the cheek. Before another moment passes, we're on the ground, rolling and kicking.

"Oh, fuck *me!*" Tess calls, throwing her hands in the air, but it's too late.

I have him wrapped up, yanking his own arm around his body so that he can't fight back. He's pinned down on the ground just as a cop and a few of the male servers appear at our side.

"That's enough," the cop says, and he shoots me a look but simply waves his hand for me to get off. It's Dayton Briggs, a face I've gotten to know through the years in our line of work. "You should probably get out of here, Waters," he says. I look up to where I last saw Tess, but she's nowhere to be found. I slide off the poor bastard, but before I stand, I kneel down to his ear.

"That girl is nineteen years old. She better never be allowed to step foot in this bar until she has a legit ID," I whisper to him. Blood trickles from his nose onto the floor. I put my hands on my knees to push myself up, but something stops me again. I lean back down to him.

"And if I find out that you ever lay another hand on her, you're a fucking dead man."

I don't know what makes me say it.

I don't know why I care so much about that part of it.

She's technically of legal age.

And then I cringe for a moment when I realize that she's been away at college for almost two years. This idiot is not the first to touch her. I feel my stomach flip.

And when you look at her, it's easy to tell that he won't be the last.

Nausea sets in.

I make a move toward the door, but I hear my name.

Fuck.

Lauren. My girlfriend.

"What the hell was that?" she asks as she follows me outside. I turn to her, too ashamed to make eye contact.

"Jackass bouncer was gonna let Tess into the bar with a fake," I say. She looks at me, puzzled.

"So?"

I swallow.

"Well, she's only nineteen. She doesn't need to be out here with these animals. I used to work here, remember? I know what kind of people hang out around here."

She crosses her arms and leans back on her heels.

"*You* used to hang out around here."

My eyes meet hers.

That's exactly my point.

When I don't say anything, she goes on.

"So, you hit him because he was going to let her into the bar?" she asks. I shake my head. When she says it out loud, I realize how ridiculous it must seem. People don't get me and Tess.

To be honest, *I* don't get me and Tess.

"Well, he kept putting his hands on her and—"

"Whoa, whoa," she says, putting a hand up. "He was handsy with her? Was she upset?"

I swallow again.

"Well, uh, no…" I pause for a moment. "I think she was…uncomfortable, but she was just trying to get in, so—"

She lifts her chin, her eyes narrowing on me.

"What...what is it with her?" she asks me. I just blink for a moment. She widens her eyes at me as if to say, *Well?* But I have no answer. Because I honestly don't know.

She sighs.

"This has been...weird. I'm gonna head out," she says as she walks by me.

"Lauren—"

"Whatever that was," she says, motioning to me and in the general direction of where I was rolling around on the floor with Blockhead, "figure it out." Then, she walks by me, keys in hand, and unlocks her car. As much as I know I should go after her, I can't. Because I don't know where Tess is, and it's freaking me out a little bit.

I pull out of the parking lot and head off in the direction of her house. I'm not sure what she's driving these days, or if she even drove in the first place. The girls she was with are still behind me in the bar. I dial her, but it goes right to voicemail.

Dammit, Tess.

After a few minutes, my heart drops when I see her up ahead on the side of the road, arms crossed over her body, the little sweater she has on doing absolutely nothing to block out the cold. My heart rate slows down instantly as soon as I know she's safe.

I roll down my window as I pull up next to her.

"Tess, get in the car, please," I say. She scoffs and just walks faster. I grit my teeth and let out a long, slow breath. Few people mean to me as much as she does, but few people can piss me off the way she does, too. "Tessa. Get in the car."

Her head flips to me with a scowl. No one ever calls her by her full name.

"Leave me alone, Cade," she says.

"We both know damn well I'm not letting you walk three miles home in the dark in December. Get in the truck."

She glares at me again.

"And we both know damn well that there's not a fucking chance I'm getting in that truck with you."

I want to smile.

I'm tough, but this girl is tougher in a lot of ways. I would never admit it out loud, but I've met my match with her.

"You're gonna make me follow you all the way home, aren't you?" I conclude. She just shrugs.

"I'm not *making* you do a damn thing. I'm a grown woman, and everyone else sees that except for, apparently, you. You're a grown-ass man. Do what you want," she says, wrapping her arms tighter around her body as she stomps down the road.

It's been a half-hour, and we're almost there. A handful of cars have beeped, a few more have crossed the double-yellow to go around me, and a car full of women stopped to ask her if she was okay. She told them she was fine, and that I was harmless, which I found funny.

I'm most definitely *not* harmless.

But Tess knows I'd kill anything that tried to cause her harm.

She has to be fucking freezing by now, but she won't dare admit it. I see her wipe her nose every few steps, her hair blowing in the bitter wind, but she doesn't reach up to keep it in place. Her arms stay tight around her, trying desperately to hold onto whatever ounce of warmth she has left in her body. In one breath, I want to laugh at her stubbornness. If she wasn't so thick-headed, she would be at home in her bed by now.

But on the other hand, I just want to grab her and hold her to me, let my heat run off on her, rub her arms with my hands to try and warm her up.

Brat.

Finally, she turns into her driveway, and I follow suit. She gets to the front door and pulls out a key, unlocks the door, and slams it behind her. Not a single word between us.

I just sit for a minute in her driveway, the engine of my truck humming. There's something unsettling about Tess being *this* mad at me. We've had tiffs here and there. But not slam-the-door-without-saying-good-night mad. And I'm not a fan. But there's something else that's leaving me feeling a little jarred. Something shifted tonight.

It wasn't just that I wanted to make sure Tess was safe. It was that I wanted to make sure she wasn't anyone else's. My heart thuds in my chest as I stare ahead at the little house I've been to so many times over the last four years.

I shake my head.

It's *Tess*. It's the chief's daughter. It's the girl we all swore to protect after he was gone. This can't be happening. But I swallow as I put my truck in reverse.

Maybe it already has.

I drive off to Grannie's house. It's only ten, and I know she is still awake, probably crocheting and watching *The Price is Right*. When I walk through the front door, she isn't even worried.

"Hi, Cadey," she calls from the living room of her tiny little farmhouse.

"Hey, Gran," I call back, hanging up my coat and walking in to sit on the couch.

"What's gotcha?" she asks almost instantly, and I smile. Gran and I, we have this connection that I've never had with anyone else. She knows what I'm thinking. She's the only person that ever knew about what my dad's girlfriend did to me when I was a kid. The scars she left on me. She's the only person that knew the hurt my mom caused.

Well, until Tess.

Once, a few years back, I was having beers and playing poker at her and her dad's house. Chief had fallen asleep on the couch, but Tess and I sat on their porch for hours, talking. And I'm not sure if it was the beer, or the moon, or what, but I told her just about everything. She just listened. She never judged. She understood why I was afraid to get angry. She got that it was because I was afraid I wouldn't be able to stop.

And when I woke up the next morning on their

couch, she had put a blanket over me and sat my boots next to the couch.

She had taken care of *me* at seventeen years old.

I remember being so mad at myself that next day. All this time spent with her, I realized how much she'd had to do for her dad and for the guys at the station. How grown up she had to be. And I had followed suit with them. Just another person for her to take care of.

But then, at the same time, there was something so natural about it. About letting her hear about my wounds. Like I didn't have to keep all my own secrets anymore. Because she was going to keep them for me.

And to this day, she has.

"That girl, Gran," I say, lying back on the couch.

"The nurse girl? What's her name?" she asks, not looking up from the throw blanket she's making.

I shake my head.

"Nah, not Lauren. Tess," I say. Her eyes jump up.

"Tess? She in town?" she asks. I nod.

I explain the whole situation while Gran just sits and nods, taking it all in. She doesn't seem surprised that I beat the living shit out of the guy. I finish the story, and we sit there for a moment. Then, Gran laughs. I raise an eyebrow.

"Am I missing something? What's so funny?" I ask.

"Maybe the problem, Cadey, is that you *do* see her as an adult," Grannie says. My eyebrows knit together. "She's a beautiful woman now, Cadey. And I think you're starting to see that."

Fuck.

This *can't* be happening.

. . .

It's the Friday before Christmas, and I *finally* got all my lights up. Decorating for the holidays is one of my favorite things. It's one of the only memories I have of my mom before she took off. How much she loved decorating. How happy it made her.

I went all out this year on both the inside and the outside. I have lights on every porch post. I have icicles dangling from the roof. I have two trees inside, all decorated to the nines, waiting for Grannie and my sister and her kids on Christmas morning. My house isn't much, but it's the place where my family—or what's left of it—comes together. And it's going to be perfect for them.

I sigh as I look down at the final piece, a wreath that Tess made me a few years back by hand. She's pretty crafty, that one. She made all the guys at the station one, personalized with something special. Our favorite colors, our favorite football teams, something special to each of us. Mine has purple ribbon woven through it, tied into a perfect bow with a wooden "W" at the center. It's my favorite thing to hang up every year. It has nothing to do with what it is or what it looks like, and everything to do with the fact that she made it for me.

I run my fingers over the ribbon, then hang it up on the door as the last twenty-four hours replay in my head.

I think you're starting to see that.

Holy shit.

I am.

Why is that woman always right?

I swipe my free hand over my face. *What the fuck am I gonna do about this?*

I take in a long breath as I stare up at the wreath, when I hear tires screeching into my driveway. I turn around to see Tess in Chief's old blue pickup. She jumps out, and before I can acknowledge the fact that she's here, she's standing two inches from me, chest to chest.

And she's *pissed.*

"Um, hi?" I say as I look down over her.

"What the *fuck,* Cade? You told them to not let me into Dilly's?" she says, the meanest, maddest look on her face I've ever seen.

I swallow.

Shit.

I take a step back from her.

"You don't need to be going there. It's not the best crowd, and you're not—"

"Don't you *dare* say I'm not twenty-one like you didn't have your first drink when you were fucking fourteen in a field somewhere."

Shit again.

"Tess, I—"

"What is it with you, Cade? Why don't you want me to have a life?"

I don't know what to say. My head is spinning with so many different emotions. I'm angry, I'm sad, I'm nervous. But mostly, I just want to be near her. "You have your own life. You have your own *girlfriend.*

Why do you have to fuck with mine? Why can't I just––"

Suddenly, I can't take it anymore. I turn around to face her again and grab her arms.

"How am I supposed to keep you safe when I don't know where you are or what you're doing? Dammit, Tess. Do you not understand that I cannot *lose* you?" I say, shaking her lightly as I speak. My whole body is trembling, and I can feel my hands clamming up on her arms.

She stares back at me, and I think we are both equally as shocked that I've just said these words out loud. And as I look down into her eyes, I realize how much she means to me, what this fear is that I've been wrestling with since I saw her at Dilly's the other night.

I fucking love her.

I want her happy. I *need* her safe. And I don't want anyone else to touch her.

Mine.

But she can't be mine. And that's the feeling that boils up inside of me.

She's the old chief's daughter. She's the girl who has grown up in front of my own two eyes. And truth be told, she's way too fucking good for me.

"Wha--what?" she stammers, her eyes bouncing back and forth between mine. I let my hands fall from her arms, and I drop my head.

I turn away from her. My heart is pumping so hard I'm worried it's going to give out.

"I can't... These past few months without you have

been fucking torturous, Tess. I try and keep busy, but I am constantly worrying about you, wondering where you've been, if you made it back to your dorm safe after a night out, wondering whose hands have…"

I hold my own up as the thought of some college-age kid who doesn't know what he's doing running his hands up and down her body makes me sick.

I don't cry.

Seriously, never. Not since my mom left.

But my jaw starts to ache, my throat constricts, and I realize what's happening.

This girl is making me cry.

"Tess, I can't—" my voice cracks.

Before I finish the words, she's on her tiptoes in front of me, her soft lips on mine. She wraps her hands around the back of my head, pulling me into her, and I'm in complete fucking ecstasy. I wrap my arms around her waist and lift her off the ground. She tastes so fucking good. Her lips are so warm against the bitter December air. The familiar smell of the same shampoo she's been using for years wraps all around me as her hair slides down off her shoulders. I reach a hand up, holding her up with one arm and using my other hand to cup her face. I stroke her cheek with my thumb and let myself melt into her.

When we finally come apart, I set her back on her feet, and she presses her forehead to mine.

"Cade," she whispers.

"Yeah, Boss?" I say, twirling one hand through her copper locks and using the other to trace the outline of her lips.

"I'm right here," she says. And then she flicks her eyes up to me, and I feel a heat building deep inside me. I pull back to look at her. I lift an eyebrow, trying to figure out if we are talking about the same thing. She swallows.

My heart is pounding in my chest, and my palms are starting to get clammy.

There's a voice in my head saying, *this is it*.

I can hear Grannie in the back of my mind, laughing and shaking her head.

Memories of Tess start running through my brain like a highlight tape—every laugh, every smile, every tear that I've dried.

And then it hits me. How much I fucking love her. How I'd kill for her. How I'd burn down the whole world for her. How I'd sit and listen to her sing and dance around the house or in the truck until I took my last breath.

On one hand, I can't believe we have reached this point, this crossroad. But in the same breath, it all makes so much sense. The way my world has revolved around her in some fashion for years. How I can't rest without knowing she's safe. Part of me is terrified to take another step. It's *Tess*. If I do this—if *we* do this—there's no going back. But I look down at her, and I know.

This girl has been in my heart for so long. And now, I want nothing more than for her to be in my arms.

I step toward her, sliding an arm behind her back and the other under the crook of her legs. I scoop her up, forgetting how tiny she is, and carry her up the porch steps and into the house, kicking the door shut behind me.

I set her down on the kitchen floor and look at her again.

I bend down to leave the softest kiss on her lips.

"Tell me what you want, Tess," I whisper.

I won't push her. I won't ruin this. I won't take any sort of lead unless it's absolutely what she wants.

I *know* what I want. I know how badly I want it.

Mine.

But I'm not making a move until she tells me exactly what she wants from me. At this point, she could tell me she wants me to walk around on all fours and bark, and I'm pretty sure I'd do it.

She takes a step toward me, and there's this spark in her eye. It's curious, almost playful.

She pushes up onto her toes and drags her lips across mine without kissing me. Her lips trail across my jaw, and I feel my dick twitch. Then, I feel her breath on my ear.

"I want you to make it so that I never forget what happens here tonight," she whispers, "for the rest of my life."

Challenge accepted.

"Yes, ma'am," I say.

I scoop her up again and set her down on the kitchen table. I kiss her gently at first, but it's like my body can't stop. It's like when you're eating an ice cream cone. You lick it slowly at first. But then it starts melting faster, the drops catching your fingers. Then once you *really* get a taste, your tongue just goes at its own speed before your brain realizes how ridiculous and ravenous you look.

That's what kissing Tess is like.

My tongue finds its way to hers, stroking it. My teeth glide across her lips, gently nipping and tugging until they're puffy and swollen. I want her so fucking bad. I want to touch every inch of her body with every inch of mine.

But something is holding me back.

And she can sense it. She pulls back for a moment and looks up at me.

"You nervous or somethin', Waters?" she asks. "Or are you still mad at me for letting that guy rub his hands all over me?"

Suddenly, I feel my spine straighten and my stomach drop. I feel her light the match.

My brow furrows, and my face grows serious.

She's egging me on.

"You think you're grown now?" I ask her. She smiles.

"Give it your best shot. I can handle it," she says, and I grit my teeth. Now she's touching the flame to me.

"You think those college boys have prepped you for this?" I ask with a chuckle. I'm peacocking a little bit, but I don't care. I'll admit when I'm not good at something. But I'm fucking good at...well, fucking. She pushes up onto her hands so that our mouths are a mere inch from each other.

"Try me," she whispers. Now she's adding gasoline.

And that's all I need. She doesn't know what she's done, but Daddy's coming for her.

I push back and stand up straight, reaching down and putting a hand on either of her hips. I pull her to the edge of the table and reach down for her jeans, unbuttoning them and tugging them down. I flip her over so her back is to me and bend her down over the table.

I tug the jeans a little more until her ass spills out of them. It's perfect and round and taut, and I want to bend down and take a bite. Then, I pull my hand back and spank her lightly.

She moans, and I salivate.

I pull my hand back and spank her again, her ass jiggling under my touch.

I grab a fistful of her hair and gently pull her head back toward me as I lean over her body.

"You think you're ready for this, little one?" I ask again, giving her one last chance, one last warning, to change her mind. But I see a devious smile tug on the corners of her mouth.

"I can take it," she says again.

I growl as I slide back down her body. I put a hand on either side of her ass and pull her cheeks apart.

"We'll see about that," I tell her just before I tilt her body up so that my mouth is on her center.

And holy *shit,* does she taste good.

She gasps as I lap my tongue slowly, easing her in gently. Her body flattens against the table, and she wraps her fingers around the edges. I lick between every fold, sucking on her lips and pulling her clit into my mouth. I'm playing with her now. She ain't seen nothing yet.

I stroke her with my tongue a few more moments, and then I grab her ankles and flip her onto her back.

She arches her back in anticipation for what's about to come, dropping her head back against the table, that perfect neck exposed and begging to be bitten. But I'll get to that.

I dive in again, my face so buried in her that I can already feel her wetness on my beard. I suck her clit into my mouth again, swirling my tongue around it in a rhythmic motion so intense that I feel her buck her hips. Then, I feel her slide away from me slightly. I lift my head up and raise an eyebrow as I hook my arms around her knees and pull her back down the table so I can feast.

"Where you think you're goin'?" I ask. She doesn't say anything, just closes her eyes and tries to steady her breathing. After another few moments, I feel her legs tighten over my shoulders, and she grabs the back of my head, pushing me into her. She starts moving her hips up and down on my tongue, and I can't help but smile as she does it.

"That's right, baby girl," I tell her. "Put me where you need me." She moans again, pushing me further into her, her nails digging into the back of my head. I feel her legs tighten again, and I know she's almost there.

"Cade, I...I'm gonna come..." she says, and I realize that she's saying it like a warning, in case I want to move, as if I'd want to be anywhere except covered by her.

"Do it, baby girl. Right in my mouth," I tell her, and that sends her over the edge. She drops her head back again, letting out a long moan trailed by whispers of my name.

I stand up and stare down at her, her stomach heaving in and out with heavy breaths, the moonlit scene on her side moving up and down with it. She drops an arm over her face.

"Sorry," she mutters, and I tilt my head.

"For what?"

She peeks an eye out and motions to my face.

"I got all over you," she tells me. And I smile. College boys. They don't know how to savor every last drop.

I run a hand over my soaked beard and smile down at her.

"That's my reward," I tell her with a smile, and she blushes. I look down at her again. God, she really is so fucking beautiful. Her breasts are the perfect handful, her nipples pink and pointed toward the ceiling. I know I just got done tasting her, but I want to do it all over again. She's my new favorite flavor. I watch her collect herself, and I wonder if she's ready to call it a night. I want to be inside her so bad, but I'd also be perfectly content having gotten her off and basking in her aftertaste.

"You ready to throw in the towel?" I ask.

She pushes up onto her elbows and lifts an eyebrow.

"You tired or somethin', old man?" she asks me. I actually laugh. I grab her hips and slide a hand up her back, lifting her gently up toward me.

"Little one, I'm about to make you forget your own name," I tell her. And she smiles and bites her bottom lip.

"Promise?" she asks. I step back from her and tug down on my own pants, snatching a condom out of the pocket before I let them fall all the way to the floor. Then I drop my boxers, and let myself spring free. I tear the condom open with my teeth and roll it on. I've been told a time or two that my size is impressive, but I'll let her be the judge of that.

Her eyes widen as she takes me in, then she looks back up at me and licks her lips.

I flip her back on her stomach and press her down gently so she's flat against the table again. I push her legs apart and lick my fingers, rubbing them against her to get her as ready for me as she can be. Then, I slide inside, and she flinches and grabs the sides of the table.

I want to fuck her silly, but I don't want to hurt her.

"You okay, baby girl?" I ask her, and she nods.

"More," she says, and I do as I'm told. I hold onto her hips and slide into her, and my eyes roll back in my head. She's so goddamn tight I swear I can feel everything.

"Damn," I whisper, and then I move myself back and forth into her as she starts gasping for air. The table is sliding slightly on the hardwood, but I don't care. I don't care if the whole house comes down around us.

She moans and yelps, my name escaping her lips and making me weaker in the knees every fucking time she does it.

"Can you take it, baby girl?" I ask her. She nods and bites her lip.

"More please," she says. I lean forward and wrap an arm under her middle, pulling her up so her back is to my chest.

"Can I have you?" I whisper in her ear. "Can I make you mine?"

She nods her head again.

"Yes," she says, her voice shaky and breathy. "Please."

I pull myself out of her and sit down in the chair behind me.

"Sit that pussy on me," I demand, and she struts over to me, climbing onto the chair. She straddles me, holding herself just above me. I look her right in the eye.

"Tell me," she says, and I cock an eyebrow.

I lean forward and pull her into me more.

"You sit that pussy on me, and you take this dick," I growl in her ear. And she does. Up and down, up and down, I watch as she takes all of me, making me disappear like a fucking magic trick.

"Oh, fuck," she says as she moves her hips back and forth on me. She lifts her hands up, one clutching her hair, the other tugging on her own nipple. "More...*please*," she says, and for a brief moment, our eyes catch. *Holy fuck*, that's hot.

I push off the chair, still inside her, and we move as

one to the bedroom. I pull out of her again and place her on my bed, facing away from me. I spread her legs and push her down so that she's face down, ass up. I lean forward and give her a quick swipe with my tongue, then I plunge into her one more time. We're both drenched in sweat, and I'm still covered in her juices, and there's something so goddamn erotic about it that I think I might burst into flames.

"Fuck, baby," I tell her, warning her that I'm getting close. But here's the thing about me. I don't like to come alone. So, I reach a hand around and find her clit, pressing down in soft and quick circles to match my own motion inside of her.

"Oh, Cade...I'm..." she says. Then, she reaches a hand up and clutches around the back of my head. "I'm...oh....oh..." And then she explodes in front of me, her body going rigid again.

"Oh, baby girl," I say. "Tess...." And then I let out an animal-like groan as I come, a wave rippling through me. She collapses in front of me, and I lean forward onto my hands. I'm seeing spots and stars and all kinds of shapes.

We lie together for a few minutes, her on her stomach, me on my side next to her. I get her a towel and wipe her off, but then I take my spot next to her again. Her eyes are closed, and she looks completely spent.

I won't lie. I'm spent, too. Not just physically, but there's something about just having sex with Tess that is making me swell inside. Like I want to spill over with tears, or laughter, or happiness. Or all of it.

After a few minutes pass, she gives me a devious smile and pushes up on her elbows.

"What?" I say.

"Round two," she says. "Before I gotta go."

And with those last words, my heart sinks.

Never once did I think about the fact that this was a one-and-done. That I would have all of Tess Connor once and then never have her again.

She wants round two, but I want so many rounds I can't put a number on it.

But if two is all I get, I'm going to make them count.

She pushes my shoulder so that I'm on my back and crawls up my body. She bends down to kiss my neck, and I feel that tingle in my dick that happens right before it gets hard.

I feel her wetness on my stomach already, and slowly, she slides herself up and down my shaft.

"What do you think you're doing?" I ask her, and she smiles again.

"It's my turn," she says. I laugh and tuck her hair behind her ear. I push up to her and kiss her softly.

"You can start," I tell her, "but then I'm taking over."

She cocks her head.

"Afraid I have more moves than you?"

I laugh again.

"I'm sure you have plenty," I tell her. "But no, it's not just that. What we just did…that was breakin'."

"Breakin'? Breakin' what?"

I smile.

"Everything. Tables, chairs—maybe backs," I laugh.

"But what we're gonna do now, this time…" I tell her. "This is makin'."

She smiles.

"And what are we makin'?"

I look into her big green eyes and stroke her chin with my thumb.

I don't say anything because she knows exactly what we're making. And if this is it, then what we make tonight has to last us a lifetime.

CHAPTER TWELVE

tess

HE ROLLS ON ANOTHER CONDOM, just as I put my hands on either side of his head, lift up my ass, and take him into me with no hands. He puts his hands on my hips as he moans, and as he closes his eyes to adjust to the sensation of being inside me again, I feel myself start to get wetter. The thought of being the one who makes him like this, who makes such a controlled, smooth man lose himself a little bit, is almost more than I can handle. But I have a lot I want to prove to him, so I can't show him that.

I move my hips slowly first, adjusting to his size again as I press my hands into his chest. Jesus, he's big.

I've hooked up with three guys since the start of the semester, which is a shockingly low body count compared to some of my friends.

Two of them were one-night stands, and I didn't come close to orgasming until after they left, and I was by myself.

The last one was a senior and had definitely been around the block a time or two.

But nothing came even remotely close to this.

I pick up the pace as he tenses up below me, and suddenly, the grip on my hips gets tighter. He lifts me just slightly and begins thrusting in and out of me with such insane intensity that I lose my breath.

"Hey," I say between moans, "this is supposed to be my rodeo."

He smirks as he looks up at me.

"You can ride me all day, then, baby."

He slows down so I regain the reins, and I lean back slightly so that he's hitting me at another angle. I swear I feel him in my stomach.

But as I start moving faster, he pushes up onto his hands and runs his hand up my back.

"Okay, little one," he says. I pause for a moment as he places a soft and shockingly innocent kiss on my lips. "My turn."

Without coming out of me, he pushes up and holds me to him, gently lowering me onto my back.

He looks down at me, his hands on the sides of my head now. He moves slowly, and I feel my breath shuddering from underneath him. He bends to kiss me again, then pulls away, running a thumb along my jawline.

"What is it?" I ask him, sensing a huge shift in the mood.

He looks down at me like he's trying to memorize every inch of my face.

"I just want to remember how every moment of this

night went, how it felt," he says. "I just never want to forget the night you were mine."

Then, he moves faster, clutching me to him as I dig my nails into his back and wrap my legs around him as tight as I can. It feels amazing, having him inside of me like this, but there's something deeper than sex happening.

This is the night where it is okay that we are in love with each other.

And as beautiful as it is, I can't help but shake a feeling of despair. Like I've gotten everything I've ever wanted, but the clock is ticking.

I squeeze my eyes shut and press my face into the side of his neck as he jerks, stiffening as he comes.

After we clean up, he lies back down on the bed and holds an arm out for me. I curl up against him as he covers us with the sheets. It's quiet for a bit as we catch our breath. My heart races as I think about what happens next. I feel that despair creeping back up, like it was a cruel trick of life to give me a taste of what was made just for me, just for it to be torn away.

Tomorrow, he'll go back to Lauren.

Oh, God. Lauren. His girlfriend. Half of me starts to die inside as I think about her. He was never really mine in the first place. But somehow, half of me knows that he was mine way before he knew about her. And I was his.

Not that it matters.

I'll finish out my break and go back to school.

But the thought of life going back to normal is too

much for me to bear. Because after tonight, nothing will ever be the same. I roll to him.

"Do you think you...do you think you'll...regret this?" I ask him. His eyes shoot to me as he rolls over so that we're nose to nose.

"Tess, why would you—"

"Because you're with someone else," I say. "And we're...we have history, and..."

He pushes up on his elbow and looks down at me, his eyes narrowed on mine, trying to get a gauge for how serious I am. When he realizes that I'm truly worried about it, he reaches a hand out for me.

"You will never know how you've changed my life, Tess Connor," he whispers as he traces my hairline with his fingers. "I could never regret you."

I nod and swallow back the lump that's been coming and going in my throat all night. He leans forward and kisses me softly again, and I let myself curl up against him. I want to ask him about what happens next. My anxiety wants to know what to prepare for. How deep the wound will be. How different we will be.

But I don't. I just lie with him, against him, letting the last bit of my soul that didn't yet belong to him jump out of my body and into his.

I wake to a soft buzzing sound, and as I blink a few more times, I realize it's his phone on the nightstand next to us.

No, wait. It's *my* phone. I can make out Aunt Marie's name, and I jump up. Fuck. I never called her.

"Hello?" I answer, trying to mask the sleepiness in my voice.

"Are you hungover, or are you with someone?" she asks. Aunt Marie and I have a pretty solid relationship. She's ten years younger than my dad, so she has always been the hip, cool aunt. She keeps it real with me, she lets me live, but she worries.

"Umm…" I say, turning to my side and realizing I'm alone in Cade's bed. "Option B," I tell her.

"Uh-huh," she says. "Thought so. Just send me a quick text next time, would ya? And don't forget we have dinner tonight."

I nod like she can see me.

"Got it. I'll be home in a bit," I tell her.

When I hang up, I suddenly feel vulnerable. I'm naked in Cade's bed—alone. I look around the room for my clothes, but I don't see them, and then I remember I started undressing out in the kitchen. Shit.

I walk toward his dresser and open the drawers until I find his t-shirts. When I pull one out, I close my eyes and bask in the scent of him. I tug it on over my head just as he walks in the door. He stops when he sees me and smiles.

"What?" I ask. He shakes his head.

"I've just…I've pictured this a few times," he says.

"Pictured what?"

"Pictured you walking around my house in my clothes. It's better than I ever could have imagined."

He walks toward me with a steaming cup of coffee and leans down to kiss me on the lips, his other hand cupping my cheek.

"Here's your bean juice," he says as he hands it to me. I raise an eyebrow.

"You made…coffee?" I ask. He nods. "But you hate coffee."

"I do. But you love it," he says. "So you have coffee."

I look down at the cup in my hands, then back up to him.

I want to ask him why he had it in the house already, if he doesn't drink it. And then I stop myself, because I realize it's probably because the other female company that joins him here are fans. But I swallow that back and smile at him.

"Thank you," I tell him. He motions back to the bed and climbs in, pulling the covers back so that I join him. As I lie next to him, I can't stop my mind from racing. Every sip of coffee I take reminds me that he already had it in his house. When I look at his closet door, I think of that time I caught him and Lauren in the closet last year. He has more than a decade on me. So much more time to figure out what he likes and what he doesn't. So much more time to please other women, to have them melting into the palm of his hand just like I did mere hours ago.

So many more women to compare last night to. So many experiences that ours must stack up against. I try all my self-talk. I try repeating the mantras my therapist has gone over with me time and time again.

We don't compare ourselves with others.
Perfection isn't real.
You had to be one of his top ten, at least.

Okay, that last one wasn't from my therapist. But I'm reaching for threads here.

Finally, I can't take it anymore. I have to know.

"What was your best time?" I ask him.

He raises an eyebrow as he points the remote at the TV.

"What?"

"Sex. What was your best time? And don't say last night."

God, the only thing worse than him telling me that his best sex wasn't with me is him lying about it out of pity.

His eyes drop from the TV to me.

"Tess," he says like a warning. Like a why-are-you-trying-to-ruin-this type of warning. But I can't live the fairytale life. As it's proven to me, time and time again, life is hard. It leaves endless scars and takes no prisoners. I know this isn't going to be real. I know this is something that has happened once, and that will be it. But I need him to tell me. I need him to say the words. I need to hear about the others so I can face the reality that I'm just one of plenty and that our time together probably doesn't even measure up to the freaky shit that some of them have probably done.

"Please," I ask again, sitting cross-legged and facing him. He looks at me again, then sits up against the headboard. He runs a hand down his face.

"Tess, why?" he asks again. But I don't answer him.

"Please," is all I say.

He sighs and drops his head back. He closes his eyes for a moment, then opens them and looks up at the ceiling, like he's going through memories like we used to go through CDs in a record store.

"There was this one time, in the rain," he says. I swallow.

"The rain, huh?" I ask, trying to sound playful, even though I'm fucking dying inside.

"Tess, I—"

"Cade, just tell me."

He sighs again.

"We had driven out on this farm one night. We had parked and were going for a walk when the sky opened up, and it just started raining buckets. It just sort of happened."

I swallow.

"So, what made it the best time?"

He knits his eyebrows together, thoughtfully.

"Well, it was just me and her and the rain," he says. "We were rolling around in the mud, just covered from head to toe in dirt and water. I don't know. It was just…sensual, I guess."

I swallow and nod.

He reaches a hand out for mine.

"Tess, why did you ask me that?"

But I swallow the lump again and shake my head. Guilt and despair both slowly creep in hand-in-hand. He doesn't belong to me. Even though I know he was mine before he was theirs, in this moment, he's not. And that realization weighs more than a ton of bricks as it settles itself on my chest, making it harder and harder to breathe. I begin to rub my chest, trying to break up the anxiety and let it go elsewhere.

"Was it with Lauren?" I ask. His eyes dart to mine. He swallows.

"No," he says. "It was before her."

I feel a tiny bit of relief knowing that his most erotic experience was with someone else other than the girl he's currently dating, but then I'm reminded that he is, in fact, dating someone else.

"Why are you asking me this?" he asks, sitting up straighter. I can't speak, though. I can't do anything but sit perfectly still, hoping that I don't succumb to the tears I feel pricking at the backs of my eyes.

But I lose the battle. The tears well at the corners of my eyes, and my shoulders start to shake. He reaches for my wrist and pulls me into his chest. He scratches the back of my head and swipes at my tears with his thumbs.

"Baby girl," he whispers, "what is it?"

I sit up after a moment and look at him.

"I just wanted to remind myself that you have had plenty before me and will after me, too," I tell him, trying to sound matter of fact. "Hell, you had someone *during* me."

His face grows even more serious, the expression on it pained.

"I got lost in us last night," I admit to him. "I needed a reality check today."

He just stares at me, trying to put together what it is I've said and what it is that I'm trying *not* to say.

I slide off the bed and walk out into the kitchen, swiping pieces of my clothing from the floor, the counter, and wherever else I lost them. I feel him follow behind me.

"Hey," he says, but I don't respond. I turn toward the bathroom to go change, but he blocks the door. "Hey," he says again.

I lift my eyes to him.

"What is going on right now?" he asks. I swallow, my eyes dropping again. He puts a finger under my chin and forces me to look at him. "Tess."

But I can't say anything. I can't bring myself to tell him that he single-handedly took my heart and broke it all in one night. And that every minute I stay here with the memory fresh, the scent of him still covering me, it breaks even more.

"Tess," he says, his voice just above a whisper, "whatever you think this was, it's not."

I don't say anything.

"It doesn't matter how many stories I tell you," he keeps going. "There is no comparing what this was— is—to any other person I've been with. There's no comparing you and me to anything."

I cross my arms over my body.

I want to believe him. But my brain is screaming at me not to.

My brain is reminding me how many times he's probably had these same conversations.

"Tess, I'm… I'm in—"

"Don't. Don't say it," I tell him. It wouldn't be the truth.

It can't be.

My mind drifts back to Lauren. The way his eyes

followed her like magnets the night the deck fell on my dad. How he drooled and ogled over her as we walked around the hospital. How they kept finding each other over and over, year after year. And how, now, he belongs to her officially. Such a strange feeling, envy. To hate certain qualities about someone, simply because you wish you had them. The thing is, I know Lauren is a good person. I know because of the way she cared for me and my father, on more than one occasion.

You're probably just his type, my brain tries to remind me. *You're just the next girl on his list.*

I know Lauren's probably good to Cade. Good for him.

He is not in love with you.

He can't be.

There's a long pause, so I take the opportunity to go into the bathroom and put my clothes back on. I fold his shirt up and leave it on the bathroom sink. I look at myself in the mirror, pressing my fingers to the hickie he left just below my collarbone.

I sigh and pull my shirt on, walking back out into the kitchen. I grab my keys from the counter where I tossed them last night and fiddle with them for a moment in my hands. He makes a move toward me, and my whole body goes stiff. I brace for his touch, for the combined feeling of home and misery.

"Tess," he says. "I…I am yours. You have me."

Now I feel something else beneath the surface. The sadness is being overrun by anger. I look at him through hooded eyes and break out of his hold.

"No, you're not," I say as I back away from him. I

turn my back to him as he follows me toward the front door.

"Tess, please just talk to me. I'm telling you, you *have* me," he says again. I whip my head around to him, my hair falling over my shoulder.

"Stop it, Cade," I say, my voice cold and stern. "I do *not* have you. *She* does. And I get whatever is left over. I deserve more than that, don't I?"

He sinks back, like he just walked into a brick wall.

Then, I turn and walk out of his door, down the steps, and, seemingly, back to my life before I crawled into his bed.

I can't have half of Cade Waters. That is the only thing I can think of that would be more painful than not having him at all.

CHAPTER THIRTEEN

cade

MY HEAD IS SPINNING as I deal with the whiplash that is Tess Connor.

I'm just standing on my front porch like a jackass, with nothing but the cold December air, the trees, and a swirling brain.

She sped off about five minutes ago, but I'm still standing here.

Last night, I had everything I ever wanted, right in my arms.

I've been hurt before. I've lost people. I've been damaged. There's a layer over me that protects me from anything happening again—or, at least, I always *thought* it protected me. But then Tess Connor came crashing into my life. And it's not even that she moved the layer back. It's that I didn't even put it up in the first place with her. It's that something inside me realized early on…I was safe with Tess.

Down to my very core. My soul recognized it was home with her.

Guns down, son. She's on your side.

But now, as I sit here in a t-shirt in December on my porch, I realize I might have already lost her before I ever really had her.

I go back inside and close the door. I walk over to the liquor cabinet, pour some bourbon in a glass that Grannie had engraved for me years ago, and thump down in one of the kitchen chairs. I take a sip and let it burn as it slides down my throat.

I think about what she said.

I deserve more than that, don't I?

She's right.

She deserves the entire fucking world.

I sigh as I pull out my phone from my pants pocket. I dial Lauren.

"Hey," she says, "I missed you last night."

I swallow.

"Hey, sorry about that. Can we meet up today?" I ask.

There's a pause.

"Meet up?" she asks. "That doesn't sound good."

I swallow, but I don't say anything else.

"Is this like a…meet-up-because-you-miss-me sort of thing," she says, "or like a meet up to break up?"

I swallow again.

"Lauren, I…"

"What's going on, Cade? We don't need to be all formal about this," she says. "Tell me the truth."

I sigh.

"Lauren, I just don't think we, uh…I just think it's time—"

"We had plans, Cade," she says. "Everything was fine yesterday. Just be straight with me. It's over. I get it. But why?"

I rub my temples.

I'm grown. I need to own my shit.

"I, uh...I slept with someone," I blurt out. "I'm so sorry, Lauren. It's...it's more than just sex. And it was always more than just sex with you. I hope you know that."

There's a long pause.

"Wow," she says after a few more moments.

"What?" I ask.

"I just...out of all the pricks I've dated, I just never thought *you* would be one of the ones who would sleep with someone else."

I swallow. There's another long pause.

Me either. And Grannie would chase me with her wooden spoon if she ever knew.

"Was it Tess?" she asks, and my eyes widen.

I don't know what to say. I don't want to drag Tess into this. Although, I guess at this point, I kind of already have.

"I, uh...why would you ask me that?" I say.

"I don't know. Woman's instinct, I guess," she says. "After the other night at the bar, when you went ballistic on that bouncer...my senses have been tingling. And when you told me just now, I was shocked that you actually did it, but there's also a part of me that's not surprised it was her. There's always been something there. Even when she was younger, you watched her like a hawk."

I scratch the back of my head.

Jesus, she's right.

"Listen, Cade. You fucked me over, and I'm furious about it. But I hope you do what you need to do to make it work with her. Before you let whatever it is between you two ruin your next relationship. Don't call me. I need a clean break from you."

She hangs up before I even have time to apologize again.

Instead, I just sit in her words, letting them soak in.

I don't want a "next relationship" unless that relationship is with Tess.

I let a few hours go by of me not doing anything but pacing my own house, wondering what my next move should be. Finally, I grab my keys and head out the door.

Five minutes later, I'm pulling up to Grannie's. It's winter, but it is a freakin' sauna in her house, regardless of the temperature outside. I quickly shake off my coat as I walk in the door, knowing I'm about to be a sweaty mess.

"Hey, Gran," I call out from the foyer.

"Hey, Cadey," she calls back, and I find her in her usual spot, in front of the TV with her crochet needle in hand. I smile. She's so consistent. Such a constant in my life. I walk in and lean down to kiss her cheek. "What's goin' on, baby?" she asks.

I sit down on the couch next to her and watch as her old, wrinkled, crooked hands move back and forth and back and forth. I sigh and brush a hand over my face.

"Gran, I need to tell you something," I say. Immediately, she puts her hands down in her lap and locks eyes with me. I swallow. "I think…I think I might be in love with…I think I might be in love with Tess Connor." I choose to eliminate the part of the story where I attempted to make her reach heaven a mere twelve hours ago. Multiple times.

"You think, or you know?" she asks me. I blink a few times.

"I know," I say, my voice low.

She smiles, then picks up her needles again.

"What's funny?" I ask her. She shakes her head and chuckles.

"You always been sweet on that girl, Cadey," she says. "When she was young, you looked out for her like she was your family. I just been watching as that slowly morphed into you being territorial."

I raise an eyebrow.

"Territorial?" I ask.

She shoots me a look.

"You tell me something, Cadey. Who do you think that girl was made for?"

I stare at her for a minute.

But a voice inside me whispers, *Mine.*

I don't answer her. I just lean back against the couch and stare up at the ceiling.

I think Grannie is right.

I think across town, in a three-bedroom ranch that

I've spent quite a few drunken nights at, sits a girl who was molded for me. Just like I was for her.

I don't need a lot of people. I'm slow to let people in. I'm quick to take care of things on my own or learn how if I don't know so that I never need to depend on anyone else.

But I need her. The same way I need air. I need her, and it's terrifying. I don't know how to need someone, but for her, I'm learning.

"What you gonna do about it?" Grannie asks me after a few minutes, as if she was giving me just enough time to get my thoughts straight. I smile and shake my head. She and I will forever be connected in that way.

"First, I guess I'm gonna find out if she wants me," I say. "And if she does, I'm gonna be whatever she needs me to be."

Grannie sighs.

"Cadey, you don't need to be anyone but you, especially not for that girl," she says.

"What do you mean?"

"That girl has loved you just as long as you've loved her," Grannie says. "Now, go get her."

CHAPTER FOURTEEN

tess

I'M IN THE KITCHEN, kneading the dough for Aunt Marie's homemade biscuits. It was a recipe of my grandma's, and it's my ultimate comfort food. After the events of last night, I'm pretty sure I'm going to need to double the recipe. Maybe triple so I can freeze some for emergencies.

Sam Cooke plays on the small radio that sits on top of the fridge. Pretty sure my dad bought it in the eighties, and it's still kickin'. I picture this thing still on Earth a few hundred years from now when humans return after we finish destroying the planet. It'll be an artifact in some futuristic museum.

I'm humming along to Sam as I scoop the last of the dough onto a cookie sheet and walk it to the oven. Aunt Marie is at the store, getting some things for dinner. Travis is coming over, a sweet new guy from the firehouse that is one thousand percent into her, but she is completely oblivious. She refuses to entertain any Dalesville suitors. But she also never talks about moving back north, either. It's like she's frozen between two lives; one she chose for herself, and one that fell into her lap, complete with a hormonal teenager she had to finish raising.

I'll forever be indebted to my aunt. To the woman who stopped her life for the child she didn't have and didn't ask for. The child she loved like her own.

Just as I'm closing the oven and wiping my hands off on a dish towel, I hear a knock on my door that makes me jump. It's more like an aggressive *bang* than a knock. I look at the clock that hangs over the sink. Aunt Marie just left a few minutes ago. She wouldn't be back yet, and if she was, she wouldn't be knocking.

I walk out into the living room, and I freeze when I see him through the front door windows. I draw in a sharp breath and walk to the door, my hand shaking as I pull it open.

"Yes?" is all I can say.

"Can we go for a drive?" he asks. I swallow and shake my head.

"Aunt Rie has a friend coming over for dinner," I say. "I'm helping cook."

He nods.

"Alright. Then, can we talk here?"

I think for a minute. I have at least a half hour before Aunt Rie gets back.

I nod and hold the door open for him to come inside.

I turn around once he closes the door and look up at him. I'm not inviting him past the foyer. That implies that he's welcome here, or that it will be an extended visit—neither of which are true.

"What did you want to talk about?" I ask him, crossing my arms over my body.

"I know we don't have a lot of time," he says, "so I'm just gonna get right to it, Tess. I have never known a love the way that I love you."

I stare at him, my eyes wide, stinging with tears that want to fall.

Don't fall for it, Tess. Don't do it.

I swallow.

"I don't know if you believe in soulmates, Tess, but I do. And yours was made for mine. You don't judge me. You're not scared of the parts of me that even I'm afraid of. You see everything, even the shit I don't share with anyone or have never spoken about. I believe in it, Tess. You can think what you want, but I know what you are and why you came into my life. And I know that even after I tell you all of this, if you don't feel the same, there will never be another love like this for me in this life. I'll just wait until it's my turn in the next one."

I swallow again, my lip trembling. I bite it to stop it from shaking, but he reaches out to touch my face, and I lose my battle. I turn my face into his palm and shake my head.

"I can't have half of you, Cade," I whisper, closing my eyes.

He bends down and kisses me. A tear rolls down my cheek between our lips, and he pulls apart, wiping it away.

"Baby girl, you have every piece of me I have to give," he whispers. "And then some."

I open my eyes as he presses his forehead to mine.

Is he saying what I think he's saying?

He pulls away, reading my mind.

"If you will have me, I am all yours, Tess Connor. And if you won't, then I'll love you from afar. There's no escaping this."

The tears keep falling, and he keeps swiping them away, leaning in to kiss my cheeks, my eyes, my lips, slowly healing the giant hole that was torn in my soul this morning. As he takes my wrists in his hands, he looks down at the bracelet he gave me last year. Some of the silver beads are starting to tarnish. He swirls the beads in his fingers, then smiles.

"Ya know, when you mix blue and purple, it just becomes a lighter blue or a darker purple, depending on how you look at it. One goes lighter or darker for the other. That's you and me. Two bodies, one soul."

I pull my arm back from him slowly, staring down at my wrist.

Two bodies, one soul.

"I know you gotta go," he whispers, kissing the top of my head. "But can I see you later? So we can talk more?"

I nod. My head is swirling, and my heart is beating so fast I feel like I can't catch my breath. He bends down to kiss me once more, and as he does, the front door opens. And I'm kissing Cade Waters in front of my aunt.

He steps away from me, looking sheepishly from me to Aunt Rie.

"Hi, Marie," he says.

She's standing with her hand on the door, looking from me, to him, to me, to him.

"I forgot my list," she says slowly, motioning toward the kitchen.

Slowly, she steps into the house and closes the door behind her, leaning against it.

"Is…is this who you were…" She points a finger at Cade but looks at me. I nod.

"Yeah, Aunt Rie," I say. "I was with Cade."

I take his hand. He squeezes it, but he doesn't take his eyes off of her.

I swallow.

"What's going on here, guys?" Aunt Rie asks finally.

I have no idea what the fuck to say. How do I tell her that I'm in love with the guy who has known me since I was a teenager? The guy who worked with my dad? Who was with me the night he died when no one else was?

Thankfully, Cade speaks up.

"Marie," he says, clearing his throat, "I'm in love with your niece."

Her eyes widen, her lips parting slightly.

"Love?" she whispers. Then, she looks at me, and I nod.

"And it's mutual," I say, realizing that this is the first time I've confirmed to Cade that I feel the way he does—not that he didn't already know. He *had* to know.

There's a long pause. Finally, Cade steps forward.

"I was just about to head out and let you all get ready for your dinner. I'll see you tonight," he says, leaning forward to kiss my head. Then, he nods to Aunt Marie and slips out the front door.

She's staring blankly at the floor and finally lifts her eyes to mine.

"Lauren?" she asks.

"It's over," I say. She nods.

Another long pause.

She walks past me, brushing a hand down her face. She reaches into the kitchen, grabs her list off the kitchen counter, and walks back to the door. Slowly, she turns around to face me.

"Look, kid," she says. "I'm not gonna tell you not to do this. I'm not gonna tell you to avoid this because you might get hurt. Because in my opinion, some of the best things in life end in hurt. So, I'm just gonna warn you, okay?" She takes a pause and draws in another long breath. "There are a lot of factors that are going to make this harder than it has to be. Your ages, your races, the distance when you go back to school."

Fuck. I hadn't even thought about when I go back to school.

"But hard is usually worth it," she says. "But here's the warning: if this ends, it will destroy you. And there's literally nothing you can do to stop it. I'm speaking from experience. It's like riding a train. Sometimes, it's a smooth ride with some sharp turns. Other times, you know it's headed full speed for a crash. But all you can do is sit back and enjoy the rest of the ride."

She walks toward me and takes my hand.

"If Cade is your crash, I'll be here waiting to dig you out of the rubble, okay?"

I swallow and nod as she pulls me in for a hug. I want to ask who her crash was, what experience she's talking about. But I don't. Instead, I hug her back, letting all my emotions from the last twenty-four hours seep out of me.

For right now, Cade Waters is mine.

I can barely sit still during dinner. I watch as Travis makes eyes at Aunt Rie, asking about where she's from, things about her childhood, what she does for a living. All the while, I'm dying to be with Cade. Finally, as I'm scraping the last of the food off the last plate in the sink, Aunt Rie joins me.

"Go," she says, reaching across and taking the plate from my hands.

"What?"

"You've basically been staring at the clock for two hours. Go. And let me know if you're staying."

I smile and kiss her cheek, say goodbye to Travis, and tug my coat off the front hook.

Within ten minutes, I'm pulling up to Cade's house.

The porch light flicks on when he hears me pull up, and he opens the door before I even get out of the car. I practically run up the porch steps, and he has me in his arms before I even make it across to him.

He carries me inside and kicks the door shut, spinning me around slowly as he kisses me.

"That was the longest fucking two hours," he says

between kisses. I smile as I tug on his bottom lip with my teeth.

"Tell me about it."

He sets me down and buries his face in my neck.

"Why'd you make me wait so long?" he moans, and I shrink back from his whiskers on my skin.

"Patience, sir," I say, tilting his chin up to mine. I give him a devious smile as he straightens up. He lifts me up and sets me on his counter, the look in his eyes stern.

"I tell you that I am completely and utterly yours," he says, then bends down to kiss the side of my neck, "then have to leave you for two hours." Then, he kisses the other side. "And you want me to be *patient?*"

"Isn't it supposed to be a virtue? Isn't that what they say?'" I laugh, remembering how my Gramma used to say it all the time.

"Little one," he says, nibbling on my neck gently, then moving his lips to my ear, "you're about to find out very quickly that I am a man of few virtues."

He pulls me off the counter and carries me to the living room. He has a fire going in the fireplace, and if I wasn't so fucking turned on right now, I'd take some time to soak in the homey feeling his house gives me.

But that will have to wait.

He sets me down on the couch, and before I know it, he's down on his knees in front of me. I swallow, remembering the last time this happened. How toe-curling, soul-snatchingly perfect it was. How it felt like an explosion inside my body that I hadn't come close to experiencing with anyone else.

He reaches for the top of my yoga pants and starts tugging them down.

"Lift," he says when he gets to my ass, and weirdly, I do exactly as I'm told.

He shimmies them down past my thighs, then lets them slide off my feet to the floor. I'm wearing a black lace thong, and his eyes flutter with delight when he sees it. He slips a finger in the side of it, but he doesn't pull it down. Instead, he pushes my legs apart and pulls me down so my ass is at the edge of the cushion.

"I have been dying to taste you again," he says before lifting the thong from me and leaning forward. He leaves one long kiss right on my pussy before he looks back up at me. "Lean back and spread." Again, I do as I'm told.

I swallow as I drop my head back, closing my eyes. His tongue swipes back and forth a few times, and then he dives in, burying himself in me. He wraps his arms around my thighs, his big hands clutching onto my ass and holding me right where he wants me. He sucks me into his mouth, swirling his tongue in a motion that makes me see stars. I reach one hand out to grab onto a pillow next to me and the other to the back of his head, pushing him into me further.

"Oh yeah," he whispers between licks. "I want you all over me."

I feel that familiar shock building deep in my belly, and as he sucks my clit into his mouth one more time, I feel my legs straighten before they fall over his shoulders.

"Jesus," I tell him as I catch my breath. "Do you

actually...like doing that?" His eyes meet mine. Before he stands, he swipes a finger between my folds, then puts it in his mouth.

"Tasting you is enough to make me explode," he says. "But seeing you like *that*"—he motions to the couch where I sit—"watching you come apart like that... That's all I would ever want or need."

I stand up from the couch and walk toward him. I reach for the hem of my shirt and pull it up over my head as I look up at him. I'm right in front of him, completely naked now. I push up on my tip-toes to kiss his lips, tasting myself on him as I do. He might have years of experience on me, but no one has ever loved him the way I do right now. I know that for a fact. And somehow, that's enough to make me feel like some sort of sex goddess. The things I want to do to him seem to be coming from some place deep within me that I didn't even know existed until Cade Waters touched me.

I drop to my knees and tug at his basketball shorts and the boxers underneath them. He's so big and hard that I feel myself getting wet again just looking at him. I take him into my mouth before he can say anything. He fills my mouth so quickly that I have to pace myself and resituate myself on him. I move my hands at his base while my tongue swirls on his head, sucking him in and out of my mouth as I do.

"Fuck, baby girl," he says, and the moans that escape him make me so excited that I can't help but go faster. I want to taste him. I want him all over me. I want him to claim me over and over and over again.

But just as he lets out another throaty groan, he reaches down and pulls me up by my elbows. He turns me around so that I'm facing away from him and pushes me onto the couch. He taps the insides of my thighs, and I spread them. He reaches up to lick the pads of his fingers, then he reaches down and rubs my clit in a circular motion until I'm practically dripping. He pauses for a minute, and I know he's going for the condom, but I reach my hand back to stop him. My heart is thudding in my chest, a combo of the thrill, and a wave of nerves. I want him inside me, but just *him*. I don't want the barrier. I want him. He pauses and I see him lift an eyebrow.

"Are you clean?" I ask, and his eyebrows jump at my bluntness. He smiles.

"What?" he asks. I sigh, my impatience getting the best of me.

"I want you without the condom," I say, breathy. "I'm clean. Are you?" I hear him scoff as he pulls my hips into him.

"I'm clean, baby girl. You think I'd let myself near you if I wasn't?" he asks. I smile. *Always* the protector. I nod and smile back, reaching around to lock my arm around his neck. He tosses the condom to the side.

The next thing I know, he pushes himself inside me from behind, and I cry out from that familiar, tantalizing mixture of pain and pleasure. Only, there's *more* pleasure. Because there is literally *nothing* between us. Just him and me. Skin to skin. Heart to heart. Soul to soul. He grabs my arms and pulls me back to his chest, and he fucks me until I'm dripping beads of sweat.

Oh yeah, we're breakin' tonight.

He's moaning my name and sucking his teeth, and he holds my hips where he wants them, and I'm pretty sure I'm melting. But then I feel him move to pull out, and I reach behind and grab his hips. He stops.

"What are you doing?" he asks.

"You don't have to pull out," I tell him.

"What?" he asks, and now *he's* the one who's impatient and breathy.

"I'm on the pill," I tell him. I turn my head to the side so I can look at him. "Do not pull out of me."

He leans forward and wraps his hand around my neck, turning my face to his.

"You want me inside you? Filling you up?"

I nod. He slides a hand forward and presses on my clit, moving in quick motions again until I'm panting.

"Yes," I tell him. "Yes please."

"Tell me what you want," he growls.

"Fill me up, please," I say. He grabs my hips and turns me so we're on the couch long ways. He pushes my head down toward the cushions and pulls my hips so my ass is up in the air.

"Yes, baby girl," he whispers, then plows into me again, moving so fast I think the couch is going to break beneath us.

"Oh! Cade," I cry out, clutching onto the sides of the couch. "Cade..."

"Oh, Tess," he says as he thrusts into me one more time, holding my hips in place as I feel him tremble inside me.

He collapses on top of me, and we lie like that for

minutes while we catch our breath. He kisses my shoulder blades, the back of my neck, and my ear gently, tucking my hair to one side.

"Yeah," he whispers with a chuckle, "after that, there's no way you weren't made just for me."

He brings me back a towel to clean off, then suggests a shower.

I have to admit, at first, I'm intimidated by the idea of going again so soon. I know women are the ones who aren't supposed to need breaks between rounds, but I can already tell I'm going to be sore tomorrow—in the best way. But still. But to my surprise, when we get in, he doesn't initiate sex at all. He pulls me under the water and lets it rain over me. Then, he reaches for his shampoo and squirts some on his hands, rubbing them together. He pulls me toward him and turns me around, and then I feel his hands scratching my head gently, massaging the shampoo in. He rinses it out, then does the same with the conditioner and moves on to the body wash. Chills pop up all over my skin as he gently cleanses every inch of me. Even when he washes between my legs, it's sensual and maybe even a little spiritual, but it's not seductive. He's truly not trying to get any. He's just bathing me. Caring for me. Letting me relax.

And I almost don't know how to handle it.

He spins me around to wash the soap off of me, and I close my eyes, letting the scalding-hot water roll off me.

"Have you done this before?" I ask. And I hear him suck his teeth behind me.

"Tess," he warns.

"No, no, I'm sorry," I say. "I don't mean to pry or start shit again. I was just wondering."

"No," he says, "I've never done this before. I'm not exactly sure why I started doing it right now, except that I just want to take care of you."

I smile to myself as he washes the rest of the soap off me and turns the water off.

A first with Cade that he's never had with anyone else.

I'll hold onto that one.

After the shower, he gives me another t-shirt of his, and we go back out to the living room. He turns the TV on, then sits down on the couch. He pats his lap and motions for me to lie down, so I do, putting my head on him and turning toward the screen. He starts scratching my head, and within a few minutes, I feel myself getting drowsy.

"Tess?" he whispers.

"Hmm?"

"Will you stay here tonight?"

I swallow. I don't know why staying through the night feels so much heavier than it did just twenty-four hours ago when I did it—when he was technically *with* someone else.

Maybe because now we've officially crossed a line. And I know there's no going back.

Cade's going to be your crash, a voice says, but I bury it.

I sit up and face him, biting my lip.

"What is it?" he asks. I stall for a moment, chewing

my lip and twisting a piece of my hair between my fingers.

"Hey," he says, reaching a hand up and taking my hand down from my hair. "What is it?"

I sigh.

"How will this work?" I ask him, motioning between us. "I leave in three weeks to go back to Salisbury. It's almost three hours away. Where does that leave us? And what do we tell people? Is this going to be too hard?"

He mutes the TV and turns so he's facing me head-on.

"Tess, I don't care if you go to school on the fucking moon," he says. "*This* works because it's supposed to. Yeah, it'll be hard. And I'll fucking hate being away from you—for five minutes, or five days, or five weeks. It'll all hurt the same. But it'll be fucking worth it every moment we are together. And will people talk? Yeah, they will. So that's something we have to be prepared for. I'll leave that up to you—if you want to shout it from the rooftops, or if you want to keep it between us. I'm yours all the same."

He takes my hand and presses it to his lips.

"Baby girl, we got nothin' but time."

I smile as I lean in and kiss him, then nestle back into his lap.

I know it's a lie. I can feel it. Time isn't expendable. It's not endless.

But for right now, I'm going to live in the lie.

Because Cade Waters is still mine.

CHAPTER FIFTEEN

tess

I NEVER KNEW I could feel like this.

So completely full. Of everything—love, joy, peace. There's worry that goes along with it, too. Worrying about him, worrying for him, worrying for us.

But mostly, being with him is peace. It doesn't feel hard. It doesn't feel confusing. It feels natural. Like breathing.

Being with him is like breathing.

It's been three weeks since the night that he kissed me in front of my aunt (who he's closer to in age than me, by the way). Three weeks since I realized that the reason I couldn't stay away from him is because I'm not supposed to.

Two bodies, one soul.

Connected in ways we don't even understand.

Three weeks, but it feels like parts of me have known him like this for a lifetime. Sometimes, at night, when I'm feeling anxious, he rolls me toward him and squeezes me because he's picked up on how my breathing changes when I'm lost in my own head. When I twirl my hair, he gently takes my hand and holds it instead.

When we're making plans, he makes them. He tells me he's taking me out and what we're eating. If I want something different, it's no problem, of course. But it's just that I don't have to make the decisions. It's like my brain gets a break from it all.

It's like my whole being has lowered its weapons and is letting someone else hold them for a change.

I haven't had peace like this at any time that I can remember in my life.

Cade is my peace.

But peace is short-lived. Like sunshine between rainstorms. Or like a big white moon before it gets hidden by a cloud.

It's only been three weeks, but now it's time for me to go back to school—almost three hours away, on the other side of the state. I leave tomorrow, and I haven't slept a wink in almost twenty-four hours. And he knows.

He's walking up our porch steps with a pie in one hand and Grannie's arm in the other. Aunt Rie invited them over for dunky balls for my last supper before I go back tomorrow. I open the door and hug Grannie first, and she squeezes me tight with her free arm. She's a tiny little thing, and that's coming from five-foot-three me. She always smells like Christmas. I don't know what it is, but every time I'm around her, I want to start belting out Christmas songs and decorating a tree.

She's the only person I know of who looks at Cade like I do.

"We gon' miss you around here, baby girl," she says to me just as Aunt Rie appears at the door to greet them. She takes the pie from Cade and bends down to give Grannie a hug. She reaches an arm around her and walks her into the house, leaving just me and Cade on the porch.

"Hey, you," he says, nudging me.

I look up at him sheepishly. I shouldn't be this upset.

Three weeks. It's been three weeks.

But all in all, it's been a lifetime.

And I don't want to leave him.

He reaches his hands out around my hips and pulls me into him. I smell that cedar and close my eyes as I lay my head on his chest.

"Two bodies, one soul," he whispers. "We're gonna be just fine. Those weeks will fly by, and we have all the weekends. Nothin' but time, baby girl. We got nothin' but time."

I smile faintly at him before he heals me with a kiss.

We join Aunt Rie and Grannie in the kitchen while Aunt Rie starts bringing the salad to the table. He sits next to me, Grannie at his other side, and we all start to eat. I smile while I listen to them all talk, soaking in every last second. This is all the family I have, but it's also all the family I need. I miss my dad always, but this is what he would want for me. Sometimes, the best family you can have is the one you choose for yourself.

When we're all done eating, I stand to help Aunt Rie get the plates, but she stops me.

"This is your going away dinner," she says. "You're not cleaning. Plus, you have plans." I raise an eyebrow and look at her, puzzled. Then, Cade clears his throat and stands from the table.

"Yes, you do," he says with a smile. I smile back at both of them, trying to figure out what they're up to.

"Go on, now," Aunt Rie says. "Grannie and I are gonna play a game of rummy, and then I'll take her back home."

Cade smiles and nods.

"Thank you, Marie," he says. He bends down to kiss Grannie's cheek. "You girls have fun."

"Bye, Cadey," Grannie says, waving us off as she piles her other dishes on her plate. Cade takes my hand and walks me to the door, grabbing my blue-and-purple scarf from the hook at the door, my hat, and my coat, and putting them all on me as we walk out the door.

"Night, you guys," I call back into the house as he pulls me outside. "You gonna tell me what we're doing?"

"We're getting dessert," he says as he opens my door and waits for me to get in his truck.

We drive in silence for a few minutes as he heads north, and I know he's going to McKellan's, this sweet little mom-and-pop place a few miles away from our house.

"Are we getting cheesecake?" I ask so enthusiastically that he starts to laugh. He nods.

"We are," he says, but then, he puts on his blinker

and turns into the parking lot of an old warehouse that closed down about ten years ago. He puts the truck in park at the far corner of the lot and turns it off.

"What are we doing?" I ask as I turn to him.

Before I know it, he's climbing to the back, his big body squeezing between the seats until he falls onto the back seat. He reaches up and grabs me by the waist, pulling through the front seats, and sits me on top of him.

"I'm gonna have my dessert first," he says. Then, he lays me back against the seat, unzips my jeans, and pulls them down to my knees.

"Cade!" I say excitedly.

"Shh," he says. "Let me enjoy mine, then you can have yours."

Then, that tongue works its magic like it has so many other nights over the last few weeks—in the shower, in the kitchen, on the floor, and now, in the backseat of his truck.

I'm panting by the end, my hand slapping back against the cool glass, giving me a total *Titanic* moment, until I go rigid, and my eyes roll back in my head.

He sits up and licks his lips, letting me collect myself.

"I will never get tired of that," he says as he adjusts himself. I laugh as I drape my arm over my eyes.

"I think you and I have that in common," I tell him. After a few moments, I sit up and get myself together. Then, I reach over for his belt, but he stops me.

"No, no," he says. I cock my head.

"Excuse me?"

169

He smiles at me and shakes his head.

"Easy, soldier," he says. "We will get to that. But we're gonna do that back home. We got some makin' to do tonight."

I smile.

The breakin' is fun. We *literally* broke one of his kitchen chairs last week when we sat down too hard during a particularly wild session. And I pulled my hamstring two weeks ago, trying to be too ambitious when I was in reverse cowgirl.

But the makin'…those are the times when I really see him. When my skin zings at every touch. When I realize that he's like air to me.

I could use some makin' tonight.

Twenty minutes later, we're eating cheesecake in his kitchen, feeding each other and laughing over old memories. And twenty-seven minutes later, we're slowly taking off each other's clothes in his bedroom. Every time I see him naked, I find something else about him that I love. His tattoos that trail down his arms. His strong shoulders that feel like they could block the whole world from me. The small speckle of hair that spatters across his chest. Random marks and scars also have their place on his skin, but I love each and every one of them. Every time I find a new one, I ask him to tell me the story. There's nothing I don't want to know about him. And when I ask too many questions, he smiles and kisses me and says, "We got nothin' but time, baby girl."

He lives his life at a slower pace than I ever have. That's what Cade has done for me. He has put his arms around me and held me still. He has made me open my eyes and take in what's around me instead of always planning for the step ahead.

So, right now, as he's trailing kisses down my neck, between my breasts, past my belly button, and down, I'm trying to live like him. I'm not thinking about tomorrow. I'm enjoying right now.

I'll make love to him tonight, and he'll make it right back.

He'll give me more of him, and I'll protect it with my life.

And I'll fall asleep on his chest while he plays with my hair, protecting me with his.

It's been almost a month since I've been back at Salisbury, and it's actually been manageable. I miss him so fucking much every minute of every day, but being busy with classwork makes it a little easier. It's the free time that drags me down, every time. Video calls and phone sex have gotten us through. I didn't think he could be any sexier, except for when he's talking me through an orgasm. I could listen to that man read a phone book—if they were still relevant.

I'm walking up the steps to my apartment, flipping through the mail while I listen to Aunt Rie talk about how she had to finally tell Travis it was never gonna happen.

"He told me he wanted to, 'take things to the next level,'" she says with a scoff. "Are men really that dense, or do they just hope you'll fuck them out of pity?"

I laugh, and she gasps.

"Oh my God, sorry," she says.

"I'm a big girl, Aunt Rie," I chuckle. "I can handle it."

"Yeah, yeah," she says. "Who would have thought that, out of the two of us, you'd be the one with the steady boyfriend in his thirties."

I laugh again. But then I freeze right in the middle of the staircase when I see the envelope in my hands.

It's addressed to me. And the return address is from a Neala Simmons, nursing department at Boston University.

"Aunt Rie," I say, my voice low. "I got a letter from your friend at Boston."

"Oh my God!" she screams into the phone. "Open it!"

I set my bag down on the steps and tear into it, holding the phone to my ear with my shoulder.

My hands start to shake as I read it.

"I...I got accepted," I say, and she immediately shrieks.

"Oh my God, Tess!" she says. "Of course you did! I am so fucking proud of you. Oh, my goodness. You're gonna love Neala. She's a phenomenal nurse. You're gonna learn so much. *And* that program guarantees you placement at Mass General. Oh, I need to call her. I'm so proud of you!"

But I don't say anything. I just feel this tightening in my chest, this lump in my throat.

This is one of the best programs in the country. I'll get my certified nursing assistant certification during the last few years of my undergrad, and then I'll be guaranteed a nursing position as soon as I graduate.

A few months ago, when I spoke to Neala, an old classmate of Aunt Rie's, I was ecstatic about this program. It was exactly what I wanted: a new city, far away from the pain that Dalesville harbored for me.

But now, everything is different.

"Are you...you okay?" Aunt Rie asks after what I don't realize is a long, awkward pause. "Tess, I know you don't want to leave him, but... Tess, this is your future. Just...think about it, okay?"

I swallow and close my eyes.

"I gotta run. I'll call you later," I say.

CHAPTER SIXTEEN

cade

EVERYTHING HURTS. Damn, getting older really is no joke. I feel like I've been living at the station for the last few days. I worked a double, and I'm so ready to take a shower and get in bed. And hear her voice.

God, it's fucking amazing how much of a difference just hearing her makes.

But as I turn on my street and look out at my own drive, my heart picks up the pace in my chest. Because she's *here*. I pull the truck in and practically jump out before I even turn it off.

"Well, *that's* officially my favorite way to come home from work," I tell her, smiling from ear-to-ear. I pick her up and swing her around, squeezing the life out of her as I do. I kiss her lips, then bury myself in her neck as I hold her off the ground. I truly will never get enough of this girl. But then, do you ever get enough of the thing that makes you whole?

I kiss her again, then finally set her back down on the ground.

"What are you doing here?" I ask her, bring her hand to my lips. She smiles, but her eyes are heavy. Something is off.

"Tess, what's going on?" I ask, without letting go of her. Her lip starts to tremble, and I feel all my senses kick into overdrive. Something—or someone—has hurt her, and I have to take care of it. She slowly pulls a piece of paper out of the pocket of her sweatshirt and hands it to me. I take it, and she walks past me to the porch steps, slumping down on them. I unfold it and start to read, and as I do, I feel my body going numb. It starts in my toes and moves it's way up, until it feels like an elephant is sitting on my chest.

"It came today," she says as I read. "I applied for it months ago and kinda forgot about it." I scan the letter, my eyebrows moving up and down, knitting together in pain.

She's got to leave you, the voice whispers. *Time is up.*

But I know I have to get it together. I slap a smile on my face as I sit down next to her.

"Tess," I say, "this…this is amazing."

She shakes her head.

"Don't," she says. I look at the letter again, scanning the words again. "Guaranteed placement" jumps out at me. Finally, I swallow and look up at her as I fold it back up.

"You have to take this," I whisper.

She whips her head up to me.

"What?"

"Tess, you have to do this," I say again, despite the voice inside that's screaming at me.

Tell her to stay, it's calling out. But I know that I can't. "This is exactly what you've always wanted to do. It's a guaranteed job. It's a new city. It's...it's perfect."

She looks at me in disbelief.

"*Perfect?*" she mutters, tears starting to form in the corners of her eyes. It's all I can do not to burst into tears myself. But I have to keep it together for her. She has to be number one. For both of us.

"Tess, you know what I mean...don't...don't get it twisted," I say. She just shakes her head. "Baby girl, I'm...I'm not going to be the reason that your whole life changes direction. I'm just not," I say. It's the truth. As much as I want to scoop her up, carry her inside this house, and keep her here with me forever, I could never do that to her.

She scoffs.

"'Changes direction?' A little late for that, don't ya think?"

I give her a look.

"You have turned my entire life on its axis, Cade Waters," she tells me. "You can't undo that."

I brush a hand over my face.

"Tess, I...I won't be that person. You're too young. You have so many decisions to make. I cannot be the reason that you derail everything. I want to be a *part* of the ride, not the reason you don't get on it in the first place."

I almost don't get the last words out. The voice inside me almost wins. I almost throw in the towel and tell her not to leave me.

But I stay strong.

She reaches for a piece of hair to twirl, and I slowly reach my hand up to pull it down. I bring her hand to my lips and kiss it softly, over and over.

She stares into my eyes, but hers seem darker than they normally do right now. We sit in silence for a moment.

"It's eight hours away," she says. "I won't be able to come home on weekends because I'll have shifts at the hospital. We won't ever see each other. How is that *perfect?*"

I swallow and look down at the folded piece of paper again.

"Cade," she says, "look at me, please." My heart splinters inside my chest.

I turn to her slowly.

"Please tell me not to do this. Tell me to stay at Salisbury," she says. A huge piece of it falls out, crashing on the pavement.

I can't feel anything. Not her skin on mine, not the wind, nothing.

"I can't," I whisper, and I bite my lip.

She stands up and clenches her fists, and I stand up next to her.

"'Two bodies, one soul,'" she says, quoting me. "What about all of that? Just bullshit?" I shoot her another look. Another piece of my heart crashes and burns.

"Don't do that," I beg. She snatches the paper from my hand and looks up at me, eyes filled to the brim with tears.

"Tell me not to go," she asks me again. "Please."

"You have to go, Tess. Your entire life has been lived for other people," I tell her. "I've had a front-row seat to it. Now, it's your turn."

She stares at me. I know she knows I'm right. I know if things were different, she'd already be packing for Boston.

Why does that happen?

Why is it that, for so long, the things we want are just out of reach, but when we finally get our hands on them, they are actually the thing that destroys us?

"But you can't leave Grannie," she whispers. I nod slowly.

"I can't leave Grannie," I whisper back. I'm all she has left, and after all she's done for me, I can't be far from her.

Just then, Tess's shoulders start to shake. Her whole body trembles, and I reach out to wrap my arms around her. I flash back to the night her dad died, hysterical in my arms as I held tight to her, keeping her steady, doing my best to hold her down when gravity had failed her.

"Shh," I say, but I feel my own jaw tremble as I hold her. We sit slowly back down again on the top step, and she lies still, curled up against my chest. I feel her reach for a piece of hair again, and I know her anxiety is winning. I take her hand and start to drag my nails up and down on her palm, drawing her focus away from the panic until she at least feels like she can inhale again. "Hey," I say after a few minutes.

She lifts swollen eyes to me, waiting for the next

words that we both know are going to crush whatever pieces of her are left, just like they will of mine.

"You're gonna go up there, and you're gonna become the most amazing fucking nurse," I tell her, clutching her head to my chest and scratching the back of it. "And then, one day, you're gonna come back here. Or I'm gonna come up there." I pull her head away from me and cup her face in my hands. "It's not our time, Tess," I whisper, and I bite my lip to stop it from trembling. I press my forehead to hers. "But I promise you that when it is, I'll make all of this worth it."

She squeezes her eyes shut and shakes her head. We both are trying to drown out the reality of having everything in our hands and knowing that we're going to let go of it of our own volition.

"Hey," I say again, and she opens them slowly. "Next time you leave your mark on that moon, leave one for me. I'll do the same. And whenever you find yourself thinking about me, just know that I'm somewhere, already thinking about you." And then, I kiss her like I'm never going to see her again.

We got nothin' but time, I always told her.

But our time ran out before it even started.

five years ago

23 + 35 YEARS

CHAPTER SEVENTEEN

tess

IT'S BEEN A FAIRLY slow shift tonight, which I guess is a good thing for Boston as a whole. I handled a broken wrist, severe stomach pain, and a major panic attack within the last few hours, but all is calm as of now.

But in emergency medicine, you get used to not getting used to the calm. I've been at Mass General a little over a year now, but it feels like I've been here decades. This job has already aged me. I've already grown so much. But I'm coming into my own. I'm really good at my job. And I feel like I'm only going to get better.

I don't run away from extra shifts. I run to them. I cover for my coworkers. I keep tabs on my patients. I get invested in their recovery, but I don't hold onto them to the point of it affecting me—yet.

I know it'll get there.

But for now, I'm riding the high.

Life's been full for the last four years. I made

enough money while I was a CNA to pay back my loans as I went, got my degree, and got the job here right after graduation. I met Alexa during my first month here, and Annie came shortly after. We found a small three-bedroom, moved in, and made it our own. It's not as homey as it could be with the three of us being ER nurses, but we grab a new plant or a candle now and then.

I don't go home much.

It's too hard.

It's too heavy.

So, I stay up here, where it's safe, in Boston. Aunt Rie says she wants to put the house up for sale, but she still hasn't. I think it's the sentiment of it all. Once the house is sold, it's another piece of my dad that's gone.

I'm shoveling down a granola bar in the breakroom when my phone vibrates on the table in front of me.

You free? Aunt Rie writes.

I pick up my phone and dial her, determined to make the most of my five minutes.

"Hey," I say between bites.

"Hey, babe," she says. "You got a minute?"

I feel the tone in her voice instantly. The hairs on the back of my neck stand up.

"What's going on?"

"Grannie Waters passed away," she says in a hushed voice. I swallow and put the last bite of the bar on the table. Suddenly, I'm not hungry anymore.

"She...when?"

"Last night. She had been sick for a few weeks,"

Aunt Rie says. "Died at the hospital. Cade was with her."

There's a long silence. Then, she goes on.

"The funeral is going to be this weekend, if you're able to come home for it. And before you even question it, you're not a bad person if you don't choose to come home, okay? Do what you're comfortable with. I just wanted you to know."

I nod to myself, trying to slow down my breathing.

"I'll be there," I say. "Is…Cade okay?"

"I haven't seen him, but I'm sure not, honey," she says. "You know how much that woman meant to him."

I let another silence go by.

"Thank you for calling me," I say. "I'll see you this weekend."

I press the "end" button.

I go back out to the floor and find my nurse manager, letting her know I have to call out for my shift this weekend. I text Annie and Alexa to see if either of them want it, and then I go back out and finish my shift, going through the motions like a goddamn ghost.

Two days later, I'm in my car, driving back down to Maryland, about to see the ghost of a man I left four years before.

When I finally pull back into Aunt Rie's driveway—it feels weird calling it "ours" anymore—she's out on the porch, waving to me. She smiles as I get out, holding her arms out as I make my way up. She holds me long and tight.

"Glad you're here, honey," she whispers. I squeeze her back.

"Me too, Aunt Rie," I say, but it's partially a lie. I want to see Cade. But I also want to avoid him like the fucking plague.

There's something so masochistic about being apart from someone you once loved—or someone that you still love. Your brain knows being apart is the most practical solution. Your body knows its limits and knows the pain being near them will cause. But your soul...your soul doesn't recognize any of that. It just sees the other half of itself and says *home*, while the rest of you begs and pleads to turn back. To stop the train before it jumps the tracks again.

But the ride will be the best of your life.

The next morning, I'm wearing a black dress, standing next to Aunt Rie in the back of the crowd at a freshly dug plot in the Grantstown Cemetery. And as I hold my breath, Cade Waters appears before me, twenty yards away, greeting people with a smile on his face. But I can see every ounce of pain he hides. The second I lay my eyes on him, I carry it for him—or at least, I want to.

My heart flutters in my chest as the pastor walks toward the casket, holding a Bible in one hand and raising his other to get the crowd's attention. And in that moment, I see what I can only describe as a blonde bombshell walk toward the front of the group. She smiles and pats shoulders and then takes Cade's extended hand, standing next to him and cuddling up close as they look toward the pastor.

It feels like I've been punched in the stomach, and Aunt Rie reaches out to take my hand.

"I didn't know he was seeing someone, sweetie," she whispers. "I'm sorry."

I shake my head and smile.

"It was four years ago, Aunt Rie," I whisper. "I'm fine."

But I'm screaming internally.

Four days, four years, or four decades. My heart doesn't recognize time when it comes to Cade Waters. The wounds are as fresh and as open as they were the day I left.

I try and focus on the pastor, listen to him tell stories about Grannie's life, about how her ancestors were some of the first freed enslaved people in the county, and how they bought the land they once worked. How they turned it into a working farm, how it's still in the family today. I try and let my thoughts leave Cade for a moment, to think about the woman that made him. The one who turned him into the man who saved me and destroyed me.

To the woman who gave us the moon.

I swallow and bow my head as he says a prayer. But as I raise it slowly, my eyes lock with Cade's from across the way. We're the only two people whose heads aren't bowed, staring at each other. All I hear is the wind. All I see is him. He nods in my direction, and I nod back, then bow my head again.

When the service ends, I tug on Aunt Rie's shirt.

"Should we get going?" I ask, trying to sound casual but fighting off the panic that's running rampant inside of me.

But as I feel a hand on mine, I realize it's too late. I spin around to face Cade Waters head on.

"Hey, Boss," he says with a smile. I can't help but melt into a smile in return. I'm the addict, and he's the drug. *A little bit won't hurt. I'll be able to walk away from this unscathed.* But as the blonde appears next to him, I know I'm only fooling myself.

He reaches his arms around me and pulls me in for a hug, and despite the fact that she's next to him, it lasts longer than I expected. I pull away from him gently.

"I'm so sorry," I say to him. Aunt Rie hugs him next, but his eyes never come off me.

"She lived a good life," he says with a smile, but I know just how good he is at pretending. I nod, my eyes falling to the woman on his arm.

"Oh, uh, Tess," he says, putting his arm around her, "this is Stevie." I wait for more of an introduction, some sort of label, but he offers nothing more.

She smiles, and it feels like birds should start singing. She looks like a princess: long golden hair that's twinkling in the sun, big blue eyes that sparkle as she looks up at him. She's long and lean and looks to be just about his age. And I don't know why, but that's the part that kills me the most.

It's not our time.

But it's hers.

"Hi, Tess," she says, sticking a hand out to me. I

take it and shake it, smiling back, as forced as the one on his face.

"Hi," I say, "it's so nice to meet you."

There's a long pause, and then, bless her soul, Aunt Rie knows.

"Well, we will let you say hi to everyone else," she says. "We better get going."

"Yes," I agree. I turn back to Stevie. "It was so nice to meet you," I say again. Then, I lift my eyes to his. "I hope you're well," is all I can manage to say. I turn to follow Aunt Rie to the car, but just as I do, I feel a tug on my hand.

"A few of us are going to Andy's tonight," he says. "Would love if you could stop by. Like old times."

I wonder, for a moment, which "old times" he's referring to—the innocent ones, or the ones when he took all of me and never gave any of it back.

I nod slowly, then turn back.

I know I shouldn't do it. I know I should keep my distance.

But I also know that, tonight, I'm going to be at Andy's.

I walk into the bar a few hours later, and as soon as the door closes behind me, I feel lightheaded. There are so many memories shrouding me that I go numb for a moment: my dad at the corner table, Rosie grabbing food from the bar, the guys cheering my name as I walk through. But none of that happens tonight.

They've refaced the front of the bar, a sleek new stone look instead of the green tile that used to cover it, and replaced all the old stained-glass light fixtures with newer, minimalist ones. It looks nice, but it feels like so much has been erased.

I turn to my left and see a group at the back table. I see Stevie, handing out drinks and chatting away with everyone around the table, like the perfect hostess. Cade is on her right, quiet and tight. I consider leaving for a minute, unsure if I can handle it, but then I'm spotted. Mel sees me and shrieks, and then, all eyes are on me.

She runs to me, and so do Jim and Dirk and the rest of the guys who are around the table. Most of them have retired, but a few of them are still there with Cade —at least, that's what Aunt Rie says.

They take turns hugging and kissing my cheeks, asking me how I'm doing, how it is up north, and when I'm coming home. I just smile and shrug.

"They keep me pretty busy up there," I say, my eyes catching Cade's.

Mel pulls me to the table and sits me down, waving to a young waitress I've never seen before.

"Get this girl a beer, please," she says. The waitress nods, and then Mel turns to me. "Tell us everything. How's the hospital? Are the men hot?"

I laugh, but I see Cade's eyes catch mine again.

I ignore it and tell her about my shifts, about Annie and Alexa, and just about all there is to know about my life in Boston, hoping to God he hears some of it. I want him to know where I am, what I'm doing. I want him to know that I'm safe, that I'm okay.

Because after all this time, I just want him to have peace.

An hour or so passes, and more people have joined. It's loud in our corner, and I sneak a peek at Stevie and Cade. Stevie is doing all the talking, making conversation with anyone who approaches. But I see Cade. I see his eyes heavy, his body sunken and tired. And I know that man. I know what he needs. I slide out from the booth and slink around to the other side of the table. I lean over so that my lips are near his ear.

"How about we go leave a mark or two?" I whisper. His eyes lighten a little when he looks up at me, and he smiles. He slides out of his chair and follows me to the back door, totally unnoticed.

We walk out the back door and into the alley behind Andy's, leaning up against the cool brick with a perfect view of the moon. We sit in silence for a minute, both of us staring up at silver.

I know he's leaving his mark for Grannie. But I wonder if he knows that I'm leaving one for him.

Finally, I turn to him.

"I'm so sorry, Cade," I say to him. "I know how much she meant to you."

His eyes are on the ground, his hands in his pockets, and he pushes a pebble around with his shoe.

"She loved you," he says with a smile. His eyes lift to mine. "She went to the grave telling me that the biggest mistake I made was not following you up there."

I swallow. This is getting heavy, and I'm not sure I'm strong enough to hold it.

I try and change the subject.

"How are you holding up?"

"No one knows this pain better than you," he says with a shrug. I nod, looking up at the moon again.

Make me strong, Dad.

"I think about him a lot," Cade says, and I whip my head to him. After all these years, like he's still reading my thoughts.

"My dad?"

He nods.

"I wonder what he would have thought about us being together," he says. I swallow. "And I wonder what he would have thought about us being apart."

I suck in a long breath.

Just one hit won't hurt, the voice says. But I squeeze my eyes shut and shake my head.

Not tonight. Not again. I turn back to him.

"Stevie seems nice," I say. He looks down at me, eyes narrowed. And he knows I'm not going to let him drag me into him again. He swallows and nods.

"She is," he says. There's a long pause. Then, he looks back up at me. "She wants to move in together."

I stare back at him, barely blinking, barely breathing.

Four years. He could have been married with kids by now.

So, why is this shocking me to my very core?

I nod slowly.

"That sounds—"

"Tess," he cuts me off. "If you tell me right now not to do it, I won't."

I stare at him, my chest heaving up and down, my palms clammy at my sides.

He takes a step closer to me and reaches for my hand.

"If you tell me not—"

"You should do it," I cut him off now. "You should move in with her."

Then, I slide my hand out of his and walk through the alley, around the building, and back out of Cade Waters' life.

CHAPTER EIGHTEEN

cade

I GO BACK into Andy's and sink down into my seat. Stevie didn't notice I was gone, but it's because she's playing hostess. I know she's doing it for me. She's trying to keep eyes off me so I can just sit. But I need to *not* sit. I need to not be around eyes. I need to be out under the moon.

Finally, I stand up.

"Hey," I whisper in her ear, "I think I might sneak out."

She looks up at me, big baby blues filled with worry.

"Okay," she says, "I'll just get the bill and—"

"No, no," I say, squeezing her hand. "I just need some time to myself. Take your time. I'll see you tomorrow. Thank you for everything, Steve." I kiss her forehead, and she squeezes my hand.

"You sure? I don't want to leave you—"

"I'm sure, Steve," I say. "Just need some time."

She nods slowly.

"Okay, honey," she says. "I'll see you tomorrow."

I get in my truck with absolutely no intention of going home. But I have no clue where I am going. I know where I want to be, and that's anywhere in the general vicinity of Tess Connor. When she's gone, I still want her. I still need her. But I can manage. I tell myself that she's happy and that her life is full, and that makes it a little bit easier. But when she's here, and I lay eyes on her, and I see what's behind them, it feels impossible to be away from her. It feels like I can't breathe.

I pull out of the lot, onto Main Street, and head in the direction of Clark Drive. After a few minutes, I'm pulling into their driveway, and for a moment, things feel eerily the same as they always have. Like I'm pulling up for a poker game. Or pulling up to drop her off.

But then I remember that nothing is the same, except that she's gone. Again.

I turn off my truck and hop out, jogging up the front steps. My heart rate spikes, but as I reach for the doorbell, it opens before I can press it.

Marie stands in front of me, her brown hair in a low braid, in plaid pajama pants and an oversized sweatshirt. I smile. Marie and I are only a few years apart, and many a time, I've heard the guys at the station talk about how much of a smokeshow she is. Marie is a beautiful woman, but she wasn't the Connor that stopped my whole world.

The one thing we did have in common, though, was the love we had for Tess.

Have for Tess.

"Hey," I say timidly. She looks up at me, puzzled.

"Hi," she says. There's a pause. "Are you here for…her?"

I nod slowly. She sighs and crosses her arms over her chest.

"She's not here," she says. "She went for a drive."

I nod again. *Fuck.*

Marie bites her lip, then looks up at me.

"Look, Cade," she says, "I'm gonna tell you where she is. But first, I need to say something to you."

I swallow. I'm not sure what direction this is going, but I don't think it's going to be pleasant.

"I knew from the second you all told me what was going on between you that you were going to be that one, that love, that derailed her whole life. I warned her about it. And sometimes, it's not something you even *do* to the other person. Sometimes it's what you *can't* do. I understand why you both had to end things. And I'll always be grateful to you for loving her the way that you did, loving her enough to let her live her own life." She bites her lip again, and I realize she's trying not to cry. "But that girl has lost more than any one person should have to lose in a lifetime. And the loss that took the most from her… was you."

My spine goes straight.

"I saw you today, with your arm around Stevie but your eyes on Tess. She derailed you, too, didn't she?"

I swallow again, looking down at her. I nod slowly.

She didn't just derail me. Her love was the purest sense of completeness I ever had in my life. And then it left me the emptiest. Walking away from her was the

195

hardest thing I've ever done. And I think I've always known it was the hardest thing I'll *ever* have to do.

Losing someone to death is finite. There are no what-ifs. There are no conditions. It's final, and the day it happens is the last day you have to do anything differently.

But losing someone who isn't dead? That's a special kind of torture. A daily reminder in the back of your mind that stirs up even the most dormant of emotions. The agony of not having them, the worry of wondering if they're okay, the overwhelming feeling of love when a familiar song comes on that you used to dance to in the kitchen. There's the confusion in wanting them to be happy while simultaneously hoping there is a part of them that will never be fully settled without you. Because if they are, then maybe it was never what you thought it was in the first place.

Losing someone by choice, even if there was no other option…that's a special circle of Hell reserved for the lucky bastards who get to fall completely in love.

And yet, in the strangest of ways, I *do* consider myself lucky because, even for the short amount of time that she was mine and I was hers, I knew what it felt like to be completely at peace. And I know now that *that* kind of peace is something that not everyone gets to experience. And those that do usually take it for granted. So, I take this pain knowingly, every day, because I got to have the peace, too.

I wait for Marie to give me a warning or to ask me not to go after her. I wait for her to tell me that if I hurt her niece again, she'll kick my ass. *Something*. But she doesn't. She reaches out and squeezes my hand.

"I'd tell you not to go after her," she starts, and I look at her, waiting for the blow, "but the truth is, either way, she'll be left broken again. Whether you go to her or whether you leave her be, I can't protect her from the storm that is you, Cade. No one can. Probably because you were the storm she was supposed to weather."

I squeeze her hand back.

"I checked her location about an hour ago. She was at some small bar up in Staub Creek. It was called Shanty's."

"Thank you, Marie," I say. I want to add something more, to let her know how serious I took everything she was saying. But I think she already knows. Tess lucked out with Marie. She was so real there was no reason to hide anything.

I get back in my truck and pull out onto Clark Drive in the direction of Staub Creek.

Forty or so minutes later, I'm pulling into Shanty's parking lot. It's a small, dingy little bar with wood posts that hold up a wood-shingled roof. The parking lot is gravel, and cars are parked every which way, no rhyme or reason. Blue light spills out of the open doors and windows and so does the soul-rattling sound of a southern blues singer whose voice is the kind that hits you right in the gut. I walk in and look around. There are a few people sitting alone at the bar, a few wait-resses making their way around the tables, and three couples dancing on a small dance floor in front of the stage.

And then I spot her, sitting alone in a booth in the corner of the bar, turned to the side so that she has a perfect view of the singer. She swirls her straw in a half-empty glass of water as she watches in a daze. She's looking at him, but I can tell she's not really seeing him. She doesn't even like country music, but she's in a trance.

Christ, she's so fucking beautiful. Even here, in this hole of a place, her hair in a ponytail that's sliding out of place, she's all I want. She's all I can see.

I take in a deep breath as a hostess approaches me, and I hold up my hand.

"I'm meeting someone," I tell her with a nod, then slip by the front in Tess's direction. I walk up to her table and break her trance, and she looks up at me, her jaw dropping to the floor.

She doesn't say anything. She just stares at me, frozen.

"Dance with me," I tell her, holding out my hand to her. She opens her mouth to say something, but I stop her. "Don't say anything. Just dance with me."

She just sits there, looking at my open hand, then back up to me.

"Just let it happen, Tess," I whisper. She bites her lip, then finally slips her hand into mine. I pull her up from the booth and lead her to the dance floor. Then, I spin her around and pull her into me, putting my other hand on the small of her back as I hold her as close as I possibly can.

Her scent is intoxicatingly familiar, sending me on a whirlwind through the past eight years. She's tight and stiff at first, but after a minute, she loosens up. She steps in closer to me, and then I feel her lay her head on my chest.

This is peace, my body reminds me. *This is home.*

I hold her tight to me, terrified she's going to slip away from me again. I lean back and reach down, tilting her face up to mine. And for a minute, we just stand there, staring into each other's core. Safe in this place, with no one we know around, no decisions to make, no pressure at all. Just us and this sad song.

Then, the song ends. She pulls away from me, like she was just face to face with reality, and pulls out of my grasp. She walks to her booth and grabs her bag, and I follow her out the door. But as she gets to her car, I put my hand on the door.

"Get in my truck with me," I propose. She looks up at me with those big green eyes, and I fucking melt. "Please."

She sighs and nods, and I lead her around to the passenger-side door, opening it for her and helping her in. She sits straight and still, facing forward, looking out the windshield. I climb in and turn the engine on, then turn to face her.

I'm not exactly sure what I want to say to her. I have no idea what my intentions were in coming here. I just knew that I needed to be with her, so I came.

I reach up and pull my visor down, and her eyes grow wide when she sees the photo that's pinned to it. The one of me, her, and her father, all those years ago.

Her smile so big and warm and genuine. I've dreamt about it. Just a short, simple dream where I'm following her, and she turns back and smiles. That's it. But it's one of my favorite dreams, one that I relive when I can't fall asleep.

The photo is pinned to my visor with the nursing pin she mailed to me when she graduated from the program last year. That's the only communication we've had in four years.

"I can't believe you still have that," she whispers. I reach up and unpin it, and she looks down at the pin in my hand. "And that. I wasn't sure you'd want it." I hand them both to her.

"It's one of my most favorite things. I keep it here in case the house ever caught fire or something," I tell her. We both pause for a moment, and I know undoubtedly that we are both thinking of her father. I clear my throat and keep going. "And of course I'd want the pin. I was so proud of you that day. I still am."

She looks down at her hands, then slides one up to pluck out a piece of her hair and starts to twist it. I reach over slowly and take her hand, holding it in mine.

"What are you doing here, Cade?" she asks, her voice soft and quiet.

"The same thing you are, I think," I tell her.

"Tell me what you want, Cade," she whispers, lifting those big eyes to me again.

I turn to her.

It's now or never.

"I want to wake up in the middle of the night and see you lying next to me, Tess," I tell her. "I want to get home from a long day of work and see you there waiting for me. I want to bring you coffee in bed and hear about your shifts at the hospital—the good ones and the bad ones."

She swallows, her eyes like saucers. I slowly rub her hand with my thumb, then I bring it to my lips. Then, I lean across the center console and tuck her hair behind her ear. I kiss her jaw, then her cheek, making a line to her ear.

"I want your body," I whisper. "I want to undress you at the end of a long day. I want to kiss you from end to end. I want to taste you while you lose yourself. I want to feel how wet you are for me, how badly you still want me after all this time. I want to be the only one who gets to bring you to the brink. I want you to come over and over and over for me, both of us knowing all the while that you're mine only. I want to be so selfish with you, Tess. And I want you to be selfish with me, too."

She blinks and looks at her hand in mine. Then, to my surprise, she slips it out.

"Why are you doing this to me?" she asks, and I see her bite her lip. Her voice cracks as she asks, and so does my heart.

"Tess, I just need you to say it," I tell her. "I just need you to tell me that it's what you want."

But she doesn't. She doesn't say *anything*. Instead, she reaches up and pins the picture back to my visor and closes it. I look at her, and my stomach is turning. I can feel her slipping away from me, and I'm starting to panic.

"Tess, am I really going to let you get away from me *twice?*" I ask her, my clutch on her hand growing tighter. She sniffs, and I see her swipe at a tear with her other hand. I reach over and turn her face to mine. "Hey," I tell her. "I'm right here."

But she shakes her head.

I don't wait for another word. I just cup her face in my hands and pull her in for a long-overdue kiss that shocks us both. I lock my hand in her hair, the other tracing her jawline as our lips crash together. She clutches onto my wrists, and I can feel the panic inside of her, too.

When we come apart, she holds tight to me for a minute, pressing her forehead to mine.

"You said it wasn't our time," she whimpers, her eyes squeezed shut like she's afraid to look at me.

"But, Tess, what if it is now?" I ask her, and I feel that tightening in my throat.

She wipes another tear, then lifts her eyes to me. She reaches into her pocket and takes something out. She turns around and holds it up, her hand shaking. And I see it's a diamond ring. She slides it on her left finger slowly, then our eyes meet again.

"What if it never is?" she whispers. Then, she pulls the handle of her door, steps down, and steps back out of my life.

present day

28 + 40 YEARS

CHAPTER NINETEEN

tess

IT'S surreal to be sitting here with him like this, after all this time. Some things feel so foreign. I've never been to this house. I've never seen the cars in the driveway. I've never petted his dog. I've only met his wife once, and she didn't know who I was at the time.

But then, some things feel so familiar, like my brain has muscle memory of exactly how to exist with him. There's a little more gray peppered in his beard, but otherwise, he hasn't changed at all. And that's when I realize that if you've loved someone, there are things about them that are branded on you forever. Just watching him, I remember how enamored I was with that boyish smile that's just a little bit crooked. That freckle on his nose that I used to love looking at while he slept. The scar on his eyebrow from his football days. The way he carried himself, the confidence of his walk, the way he was so aware of everyone around him and what they needed. All these things feel the same, like they have been preserved for me for this moment.

But they're not the same. Time has passed, vows were said, cancer has infiltrated his body and now his life.

"So," he says. "Tell me what I missed over the last five years."

I just look at him, and I can't help but smile at how casual he is.

He's dying, but he wants to know what I've been up to.

We were in love once, but he wants to know what I've been up to.

"Before we do that, why don't you tell me a few things?" I ask, leaning back in my chair and crossing my arms.

"Uh-oh," he laughs as he sets his glass down. "Am I in for an old-school Tess interrogation?"

I smile and shrug.

"Maybe," I say.

"Okay, okay." He smiles and holds his hands up. "What do you want to know, Boss?"

"First of all, how are you?" I ask, and his eyebrows knit together for a split second while he considers how he's going to answer what should be the most basic question. But for him, the complicated man sitting in front of me, it will be one of the hardest to answer.

He shrugs his big, broad shoulders. He still looks like himself. Maybe a few more lines around his eyes. But he's still my Cade. His bourbon, honey-colored eyes. His soft smile.

"I'm always gonna be okay," he tells me, but he's

not smiling. His face is serious, his eyebrows still tugging together. I stare back at him.

"I still hate when you say that," I tell him, and he finally cracks a little smile.

"Had to see if you were gonna let me get away with it at least once," he says with a chuckle, and I can't help but smile back at him.

"At least twice," I say, and he stops and looks right at me again, smiling and shaking his head.

"You don't forget anything," he says.

"Sure don't. Now, how are you? Actually. Don't try and hide from me, Cade Bryce Waters. You know I can see right through it," I say. He sucks his teeth and sits back in his chair.

"Wasn't sure if, after all this time, you still could," he says. I tilt my head up a little bit.

"Doesn't seem to have gone away."

We sit in silence for a moment before he answers.

"I'm... It is what it is, ya know?" he says, and I feel the frustration boiling in my belly. Or maybe it's not frustration. Maybe it's the fact that I've been internally screaming for three days since Stevie called me because he's dying, but he's sitting here in front of me, cool as a cucumber. But just like I can read him, he can read me. And he knows I won't be satisfied with that response. "I can't control it. I can't do anything else about it now."

"Is that the truth?" I ask. "The doctors are saying there's nothing that can be done?"

He shrugs.

"There are things we can 'try,'" he says with air

quotes, "but I don't know that I want to spend the time I have left 'trying' things that may or may not make me more miserable than this fucking cancer. I just want…"

His voice trails off, and his head drops. He looks down at his hands folded on the table.

He lifts his eyes to me, and I can see they've glassed over. There's a long, drawn-out pause, and for a moment, I recognize this face, because I've seen it before. It's the face he makes before he's about to cry, and I know that if he does, I will, too. Working in emergency medicine for the last few years has made me even more of a robot than ever. I don't cry. When I have a bad shift, I blast music, I run, and I watch *Smokey and the Bandit*.

I haven't cried in the last five years—since the last time I laid eyes on Cade. I think, after that night, I let go of every tear that could have possibly been left in my body.

I haven't cried in five years, but if he cries, I just might break that streak.

Because the only thing capable of breaking me, is watching the man I broke before, break all over again.

My voice cracks as I try to speak.

"What do you want, Cade?" I manage to whisper. He looks back up at me, a smile on his lips.

"I want to take you up into the woods."

CHAPTER TWENTY

WE'VE BEEN WALKING for about ten minutes, and I see my favorite spot about a hundred meters ahead of us. It's this big, flat boulder covered in moss that sits in the middle of the trees, like a stage of some sort. It's far enough from the house that you can't hear anything up here. No traffic, no people. Just me and the trees. And now Tess. Which is funny because, so many times, I've pictured exactly this. Sharing this spot with her. No one else has been here with me. Not even Stevie.

"There it is," I say, motioning to it. She looks up ahead and nods. We finally reach it, and I lean up against it, taking a break. She does the same, only, she doesn't seem to be as out of breath as I am.

"This is the spot, huh?" she asks as she looks around. I nod.

"This is it," I tell her. "My own personal church of sorts. I do my best thinking here." Then, I look at her.

"Usually a good view of the moon from this rock, too. So, I leave my best marks."

She nods slowly, her eyes lifting up to the blue sky above us.

"I leave mine, too," she says. "So, tell me everything."

I smile.

"Everything, huh?"

She smiles back and nods, pulling her legs up onto the rock and tucking them under her.

"Well, the guys are good. Dirk finally retired about two years ago. So, from the original crew, it's just Jim and me. Mel has one more year, she says, but we will see. You know she lives and breathes for that place."

She smiles and nods. "Yeah, she does," she says. "And you? Heard you made chief."

I nod.

"Big shoes to fill, I know," I tell her. "But I try and make him proud."

She looks up at the sky again.

"He is."

"So, what about you?" I ask her. "Your turn."

She draws in a long breath and rubs her hands on her thighs.

"Oh, uh, not much to tell," she says with a shrug. "I'm a nurse manager in the ER now. I work way too much and do very little else."

I smile.

"But do you like it?" I ask her. She nods.

"I do."

"Then, that's all that matters," I say. "So, are you living, uh, in the city or—" I stumble over my words, hoping desperately that she picks up what I'm putting down. She smiles at me, and suddenly, I know she does.

"I live in an apartment with my two best friends from the hospital, Annie and Alexa. You'd like them."

I smile and nod slowly, taking it all in. My eyes drop to her bare hand again, but like always, she reads my mind. She holds up her hand and wiggles her finger.

"I didn't go through with it," she says. "His name was Elijah. He was…fantastic. I mean, honestly. He was kind and caring and just…genuinely interested in me."

"Sounds picture perfect," I say, and I don't mean it to sound as sarcastic as it probably does. But she just smiles.

"He was. But I'd sit there sometimes and think about how foreign I felt in my own life with him. He had all these great plans for us: buying a house, moving together out to the suburbs. But I would just sit there sometimes and think, I didn't leave home, I didn't…I didn't leave…I didn't rob myself of…whatever *this* was…to feel like a stranger in my own life. I don't know. Most people didn't get it, but I did. And honestly, I'm not really interested in being anything other than a Connor, anyway."

I think for a minute, processing all she's saying.

I get it because I feel it. Stevie and I…we're comfortable with each other. After all this time, it makes sense. We get through things well together. We're each other's biggest cheerleaders.

She's my best friend. But every night, I wait for the void to be filled. And it never is.

I look at Tess, taking her in. I know this might be it. This might be the only chance I have to say it all.

"All these years, Tess, when I come up here and I leave my mark, I'm not talking to Grannie, or to my dad, or yours."

She narrows her eyes at me.

"I'm talking to you. Every single time," I tell her. "And since we got the news a few weeks ago, I've come up here every single night, praying to God, or whatever it is that's up there, that somehow you'd hear me. The truth is, I was terrified to leave you, and I didn't even have you."

She's still for a moment, then looks up at me.

"Well, I can hear you now," she says. "So, what is it you want to say?"

Just then, we hear Buster barking back at the house, and I know someone's coming up that driveway. More than likely, that someone is my wife.

We walk back through the woods, and as much as I hate to admit it, I'm wiped. My body hurts all over, joints, muscles, even my skin. I hate the idea that there is something inside of me that might be stronger than I am. But I shake my head and go about my evening, dealing with it the same way I've been dealing with it since I got the diagnosis—by not dealing with it at all.

When we get back down to the house, I can see the kitchen light on. I check the time on my phone, and I know she's probably making dinner.

When we get back to the driveway, Tess takes a step toward her car.

But before I can stop her, Stevie does.

"You leaving already?" she asks from the porch. She's dressed in jeans and a flannel, and I always loved how cute she looked in those. Tess turns to her.

There's something so wild about the duality of this situation. About the two women I've spent most of my adult years loving. About the two women who molded me into the man I am. Different versions of myself, each of them. But myself, nonetheless.

"Oh, yeah. I was gonna head to my aunt's and let you all have dinner," she says, nervously tucking a piece of hair behind her ear.

"Oh, alright," Stevie says. "I was hoping you'd stay for dinner. Will you be in town for a while?"

I turn back to Tess. She swallows.

"It's sort of open-ended," she says. Stevie nods.

"How about dinner tomorrow, then?" she asks. Tess swallows again, looking from Stevie to me.

"Uh, yeah, sure," she says, "that would be great."

She says goodbye to us both, gets in her car, and drives away.

I silently thank the gods above that my wife invited her back. I thought seeing Tess again would bring me closure. But the truth is, I feel more like an open wound after that short reunion than ever. And it has nothing to do with cancer.

I watch her pull away, then I walk the porch steps and follow Stevie into the kitchen. She's already back at the stove, stirring away at something in her stock pot that has the whole house smelling like heaven.

"Mmm," I say as I walk behind her. "What's it gonna be?"

"Gnocchi soup," she says curtly, then shakes some salt in the pot and keeps stirring. I try and think about what to say next, but I'm drawing a blank, which is a weird feeling to have with the person you've been sharing your life with. Like you're strangers in your own house.

I sit down at the table and begin flipping through a pile of mail that sits in front of me. She puts the ladle down and looks up at me.

"You need to make a decision this week," she says, her voice low and steady.

I look up at her, my body still. *A decision?* Is she asking me to decide between her and—

"Please, Cade. If you decide to do nothing, then I can't stop you. But you have to decide one way or the other. We need to let Doctor Sang know. And we need to… I just want to be prepared."

Then, she turns the stove off, puts the lid on the pot, and walks out of the room.

I blow out a sigh of relief as I sit there alone in our kitchen.

I'd rather make a decision about whether or not I want to live or die than have to decide between hurting my wife and choosing to let Tess go again.

CHAPTER TWENTY-ONE

tess

"SO, WHAT HAPPENED?" Aunt Rie asks as she puts the glass of much-needed Merlot in front of me. I take a long swig and put it back down, rubbing my temple with the other hand. She pulls out the chair at our small, circular kitchen table and sits with me.

"I mean...not a whole lot," I say with a shrug, tracing the top of my wine glass with my finger. "She left right after I got there, and then he and I just...talked."

She raises an eyebrow, and I roll my eyes.

"Seriously. We just talked," I tell her. "And then she got home and invited me back for dinner tomorrow."

Aunt Rie's eyes widen as she takes a sip of her wine and sets it back down.

"She invited you *back?*" she asks. I nod.

"I have no idea what to do," I say.

"Well, what did you tell them?"

"I said yes," I say. "I mean, what was I supposed to do?"

She thinks for a minute.

"Yeah," she says. "That's just…awkward as fuck."

I chuckle.

"You're telling me."

There's another long pause.

"Ugh," I say, burying my face in my hands. "What am I doing here, Aunt Rie?"

She reaches across the table and squeezes my wrist.

"Honey, you and I both know that if you shouldn't be here, you wouldn't be." I look up at her. "This is a new one, I've gotta say. But honey, you owe it to yourself to see this through. To try and get *some* kind of closure. Because in a few months—or weeks? I'm not sure—you could have…" Her voice trails off, and I know what she's trying to tell me.

She's trying to tell me to make the most of this opportunity of time with Cade. Because soon, it won't be an option. Soon, that cancer is going to take away the only man who ever mattered. And all that will be left for me to do is wish that I had taken the time to be around him instead of watch those wasted years go by.

She stands from the table and leans over to kiss the top of my head.

"My sweet girl," she whispers. "I hate how hard life has hit you. Over and over. And if I could take all the blows for you, I would. But the way you stand back up doesn't go unnoticed by me."

I close my eyes and squeeze her hand as she says goodnight and makes her way upstairs. I've said it before, and I'll say it again. I lucked out with Aunt Rie. I follow behind her, up to my old room, and it's like walking into a time capsule when I turn on the light. The light-aqua color of the walls, the sheer curtains on the window, my gold-framed bed in the middle of the room, still in place after all these years.

I sit down on the bed, take in a long breath, and then I cry. I cry for the time we had. I cry for the time we lost. I cry for the time we will never have. And I cry for the time that's left, knowing it won't even be close to enough.

The next night, Aunt Rie kisses my cheek and waves goodbye to me as she peels out of the driveway, off to meet Mel for a girls' night in D.C. I watch her disappear, then I lock the front door behind me and get in my own car, headed in the direction of Cade and Stevie's house in Grantstown. Twenty minutes later, I'm pulling back up the same long driveway, parking in front of the picture-perfect farmhouse they live in together. I draw in a sharp breath and get out. As I raise my hand to knock on the front door, it opens. Stevie stands there with a smile, but to my surprise—and confusion—she steps out and pulls the door closed behind her.

"Hey," she says. "Cade's sleeping. He wasn't feeling well earlier, and I don't want to wake him. Do you mind if we just chat for a bit until he wakes up? Dinner will be ready soon."

I swallow.

I wasn't looking forward to the awkward situation

of being with his wife when Cade was going to be there as a buffer. So, I'm *definitely* not looking forward to it without him. But I smile and realize quickly that I don't have another option.

"Oh, yes," I say. "Of course. No problem."

She smiles and leads me around the wrap-around to the side of the house. There are other houses in the distance, surrounded by trees that leave the rolling hills in a blanket of red and gold. She leads me to two wooden rocking chairs and holds her hand out.

"This okay?" she asks.

I smile and nod.

"This is perfect," I lie. We sit down and look out over the picturesque fall scene in front of us in silence for a moment. "This is beautiful," I finally say.

She smiles and nods.

"Thank you," she says. "My grandparents owned that house over there," she says, pointing to a smaller farmhouse in the distance. "This was all their land that they sold off through the years. There was one lot left when Cade and I were looking to build a few years back, and we snagged it."

"Oh, wow," I said. "That was meant to be, huh?"

She nods.

There's a long pause, and I watch her eyes drop down to her hands that she's rubbing together enough to start a fire.

She turns to me slowly, her eyes narrowing on mine.

"Are you in love with my husband?" she asks.

I swallow, staring at her blankly, unsure if I heard the words correctly.

But she sits straight and still, staring at me, waiting for a response, and I know that I did.

I clear my throat and look at her, sitting back in my chair. I want to say something, but words are failing me. Air is failing me. *Everything* is failing me—including my own fucking body. I feel that weight on my chest, my palms clamming, my cheeks on fire. She takes in a long breath and closes her eyes.

"Look, Tess," she says, "don't bullshit me, okay?" She stands from her chair and walks to the railing, putting her hands on it and looking out over the valley. "I'm sick of the tip-toeing. Of the people around me pretending like this whole scenario with him doesn't end in fucking agony. I don't need a bunch of people babying me. I need *truth*. I don't need people telling me how strong I am. I know I'm strong. Otherwise, I wouldn't have called *you*."

I swallow again, rubbing my hands on my thighs before pushing myself to stand. I look at the woman in front of me. It's so easy to see how anyone, even Cade, could be in love with her. She is summer embodied. She's warm and sunny, both in looks and personality. I know she's closer to Cade's age than mine, but she rivals girls my age in every way. There are lines by her eyes, but they make her look happy, not old. I know from social-media stalking and from catch-ups with Mel that she's worked as the county's public information officer for almost twenty years, and she's won all kinds of awards for her work. That's how she and Cade met. I know she's got drive, and I know, as much as it pains me to admit it, that she's made Cade happy.

And I know, judging by the way she's breathing, how straight she's standing, how white her knuckles are turning from squeezing the rail, that she loves him. And now, she's about to lose him.

She deserves the truth.

I stand up and walk toward her.

"Okay," I say. "No bullshit." My heart is beating so hard I can hear it in my ears. "I've loved him since the day I met him, and I will love him long after I die. He's a part of me."

She turns to me slowly, and I see the tears welling in the corners of her eyes. My heart is breaking for her, for Cade, for myself. I hate being this person, but I won't be one more person who sugarcoats things for this woman. If I were her, I'd want the truth too, no matter how much damage it did.

Her lip starts to tremble, and I notice out of the corner of my eye that her hands are shaking. She takes a step back from me, and I have no idea what the fuck to do. I'm pretty positive that I'm the last person she wants a supportive hug from.

"I..." she says, her voice cracking. "I can't believe that, after all of this, and everything I've been through with him...I can't believe it ends with you."

I swallow, my eyebrows knitting together. I watch as she walks back to the chair and sits down, laying her head back slowly against the wood. I sit back down and turn to her.

"Stevie," I say, trying to collect my thoughts. "It

may have started with me, but it's ending with you. You are his rock. His goal. Just because we have love doesn't make the love between you two any less real. You're his partner. I'm just—"

"You're the one that got away. And I didn't even know it at the time, but I'm the one that picked up the pieces in the aftermath. And now, you'll leave. And then he'll leave. And no one will be left to pick up mine."

I'm about to speak when Cade appears from around the corner of the house.

"What's going on?"

CHAPTER TWENTY-TWO

cade

I'M STANDING on my porch with my wife *and* the girl who I'm pretty positive is the love of my life.

I realize how completely fucked that sounds, and I wish I could make it sound better. More humane. But my time is running out, and I can't. I freeze in place when I see them, both looking like they've seen a ghost, and Stevie with tears in her eyes.

"What's going on?" I ask, still in a haze from my sleep.

Stevie stands and clears her throat. She swipes at the tears quickly, then walks past me and Tess, back to the front door. I look over at Tess, who is sitting on the rocking chair on the porch with her hands clasped between her legs. I walk toward her.

"What just happened?" I ask.

She looks up at me and bites her lip.

"She asked me if I'm in love with you," she says. My heart stops beating in my chest for a moment.

"What...what did you tell her?" I whisper. She stands up and crosses her arms over her chest.

"I told her the truth," she says. "I'm sorry, Cade." Then, she breezes past me and back down the porch steps to her car. I brush a hand over my face and walk to the edge of the porch steps, my head and my heart pulling me in two different directions. But I sigh as I turn to walk back into my house.

"Steve?" I call out as I walk through the foyer. She's not in the kitchen, and I walk in and turn off the oven, knowing that we won't be eating for a while, if at all now. "Steve?"

I stop searching when I find her in our bedroom, sitting on her side of the bed, her back to me. She's looking out the window, as still and stoic as a statue, and my first reaction is to run and hold her. But I know, right now, that would do more damage than fix anything. I walk across the room and kneel down in front of her. I put my hands on her legs and look up at her, willing her to look back at me. Finally, she does.

"Talk to me, Steve," I whisper. I slide my hands up to cover hers, but she jerks them back. The look in her eyes is one of disdain and such a deep sadness that I feel my insides churning. I'm a fixer, but I think I'm the one who broke this. "Steve," I whisper as I push up onto my feet. I sit down next to her on the bed and put my arm around her, but she slides out of my reach.

"Five years," she finally says, her voice cracked and broken. "That's not a small amount of time, Cade." A single tear rolls down her cheek, but she makes no move to wipe it away. "She's the one you're supposed to be with, isn't she?"

I swallow.

"Steve, I—"

"Please," she says, "for the love of God, just tell me the truth. Don't leave me on this planet, wondering if I ever meant anything to you at all."

I feel the air being sucked out of my lungs. I have a massive headache, and this isn't exactly easing the pain. But I will take all the pain in the world so that my people never have to feel it.

"Steve, is that why you invited her here?" I ask. She thinks for a minute, tears still streaming down her face.

"Partially," she admits. "Selfishly, I invited her here because I never understood what it was that she meant to you. And I couldn't imagine losing you before I had the answers. But I also invited her here because, in the worst-case scenario that my gut instincts were right, I couldn't bear the thought of you never seeing her again. I love you too much to keep that from you. No matter how much it absolutely destroys me."

I reach out and take her into my arms before she has the chance to pull away. I pull her into me, clutching her head to my chest.

"Jesus, woman," I whisper to her as I try my damndest not to cry, "you love me so well."

She lets out a tiny sob, and it breaks me.

"I love you, Steve," I say, and I mean it with every fiber of my being. I love her so much. But as the words leave my mouth, I feel her pulling back. She lifts those baby blues to me, swollen and bloodshot.

"Loving me isn't enough, Cade," she whispers. "You have to *want* me, too. I don't want to be *anybody's* second choice. But especially not my husband's."

I stare into her eyes, our chests falling and rising in unison. I feel the blood rushing through my body, burning as it flows. She stands up from the bed and takes a few steps back from me. Her eyes are moving from side to side, like she's calculating her thoughts and getting them together. I brace myself for the blow.

Finally, she looks up at me.

"Cade, I love you," she says. "And until this moment, I thought I knew what it meant to have someone who was my soulmate. I realize now that that's only because I've never experienced it with anyone else. Not the way you have with her."

I can't move. My feet feel like they're nailed to the floor.

"Just tell me one thing," she says, and I swallow. "Was any of it real? Or did you know the whole time you were with me that you were supposed to be with her?"

Fuck.

I let my eyes fall for a moment, but I pick them back up to meet hers. *Be a man, Waters.*

"Steve, I never once lied to you when I told you I loved you. I always have, and I always will. You gave me something that no one else in my life ever had. You gave me stability. You gave me somewhere I could put my feet down and plant roots."

She nods her head.

"That doesn't really answer my question, Cade," she whispers. I brush a hand over my head.

"I knew I was supposed to be with her, Steve," I whisper back. "But I knew I couldn't be. So, I loved you as best I could, with everything I had left."

She pauses for a moment, her eyes moving back and forth across the hardwood.

"The stability you mentioned...she didn't give you any of that?" she asks. I shake my head.

"Honestly, no. With Tess, it was a bit tumultuous. We never got to just be settled for too long."

She's quiet again, eyes still scanning the floor like she's trying to make pieces fit.

"And yet, she's still the one you want."

I don't respond.

Fix it, my brain is screaming. But my heart knows I can't. She draws in a long, shaky breath, then something about my wife changes. She goes from completely broken, to completely machine right before my eyes. She doesn't look at me, but she starts to speak.

"I will stay married to you. For all intents and purposes, I will be your wife. You will stay on my insurance. We will keep the mortgage. If you decide to do treatment, I will be there, waiting by your bedside, if you want me to be. I won't complicate your life more than it already is. But I need to fall out of love with you. Everything has changed. So, I absolve you of this marriage. And I absolve myself of it. Because I deserve more."

She stands up slowly and walks toward the door, and I've gone completely numb.

She turns to me.

"I want to be with you for the hard stuff, if that's okay. The appointments, whatever you decide to do, I want to be there. Because I can't even begin to sift through my feelings right now, but I do know that if you're gone in a year, I will never regret being with you for that time." She pauses for a minute, and although she is effectively ending our marriage, she seems calm and oddly steady. "Call her, Cade. Be with her. I'll never ask you about it, and from this day forward, you owe me no explanation. But you *do* owe me time and space. So, I'm going to take that." As she turns to walk out the door, I feel the panic kick in. My instinct is to call to her, tell her she's wrong, tell her I want to be with her.

The fixer in me wants things to be right for *her*. But doing that would continue to perpetuate the lie I've been living for five years. The massive misconception that I've been trying to get myself to fall for since Tess got out of my truck that night.

That I'm okay without her. That I live every day, instead of merely surviving. That I don't think about her in my happiest of victories, the deepest depths of my losses, and every damn thing in between.

And yet, with my clock ticking, I've never been more sure that Stevie is right. I've never been more confident in my decision to let her walk out that door, and that our time together has come to an end.

Even if Tess denies me, even if she refuses me, and even if I die tomorrow, I don't want to spend another day lying to myself or to the people around me—people who love and care about me—that I'm fulfilled. I'd rather live out my last days alone than choose anyone else over her. It's my time, and for once in my life, I'm going to be selfish with it.

Stevie is a casualty that I will take to my grave. And yet, I also feel a strange peace about it. Because I know how absolutely amazing she is. And I know that some man, who is way better than I am, is going to come around and love her better than I ever could.

So instead, I walk toward my wife and grab her hand. I spin her around to face me, but she won't lift her eyes to look at me. I take her other hand in mine, and I pull her into me.

"Steve, I...I don't know exactly what to say to you," I tell her. "Because I won't lie to you. Or to myself. So, instead, I'm just going to thank you. For loving me the way you did. For being by my side."

Slowly, she lifts her eyes to me. Then, she pulls her hands from mine.

"You were an amazing husband, Cade," she says. "But I deserve to be somebody's Tess."

Then, she walks out the door.

CHAPTER TWENTY-THREE

tess

IT'S BEEN ALMOST two hours since I walked off that porch, and I swear, my heart is still racing. I feel faint as I pull into the parking lot of Shanty's and put my car in park. It's rainy, cold, and dark, except for the blinking light of an ancient streetlight on the corner and the familiar blue light from the neon signs that bounces off the puddles on the pavement.

I've come back to Shanty's twice since the last time he found me here.

Once was when I came home for Christmas, and Aunt Rie told me Cade and Stevie were engaged.

The next was when I was back for a weekend, and she told me they had gotten married.

I never went in. I just sat in the parking lot like I'm doing right now. My last memory of the inside of the bar was when I was in his arms, breathing him in, letting him hold me, right before we broke each other again.

But before the break was fucking beautiful.

I don't want anything to disturb the memory, so I leave it be. I just sit outside, trying desperately to relive it.

I keep replaying the last few hours in my head.

How I broke that woman's heart.

How I watched her come to an earth-shattering realization. Except, it felt more like a confirmation. Like somehow, she had always known.

How, for the first time in my life, I was selfish with my own truth when I told Cade that I was still in love with him. I turn the engine off and sit back against my seat, staring at the raindrops that slide down my windshield. I close my eyes and try my best to travel back to that night, here at Shanty's. I try to recreate it from memory, the emotionally crippling song that was playing, the shock I felt when he appeared at my side, the instant feeling of home when he pulled me up from that booth and into his arms.

But my memory is short-lived when my phone vibrates against my cupholder, making an awful grinding sound that makes me jump. I freeze when I see his name flash on my screen. It's been so long since he's called.

I don't know what to do. On one hand, I want nothing more than to hear his voice. On the other, I am terrified he's calling to tell me that I've ruined his life— or what's left of it. And that's what's been haunting me the most since I ran off that porch. The thought that I maybe should have kept my mouth shut. That I should have taken it with me to the grave so that he could have lived the rest of his life in peace.

It keeps ringing, and I finally slide the green button and put it to my ear.

"Hello?" I answer sheepishly.

"Where are you?" he asks, and I can't get a read on his tone or mood.

"I'm, uh, in my car," I say.

"Tess, where is your car?"

I pause.

"I'm, uh, outside of Shanty's."

"I thought you might be, since you weren't at any of the usual spots. I'm on my way. Please don't leave."

Before I can ask any questions, he hangs up. So, I put the phone back down and lean back against the seat again. I slide one hand up and start twisting a piece of my hair. I debate going inside to get a drink to calm my nerves, but I won't risk changing the memory. So, instead, I just sit here in my car, quietly in the fall rain, waiting for my fate.

Twenty minutes later, I hear the rumble of his truck as it backs into the spot next to me, and my stomach twists and turns into a thousand knots. I wait as he turns off the engine, gets out of his truck, and pulls on my passenger handle. He slides into my car, and I want to smile at how squished his knees are against my dash. All six-foot-four of him, crammed into the front seat of my tiny little sedan. But I have no idea what's about to happen here, so I can't bring myself to do it.

He turns to me as he wipes the raindrops from his brow.

"Tess," he finally says, and I swallow. "I could walk into that appointment next week, and I could find out that I have days, weeks left."

My heart is racing so hard that my chest hurts. *My* world without him was unbearable. But the *entire* world without him would be suffocating.

"Or maybe I'll find out I have years," he says. "But either way, I want to spend it with you. Whatever time I have left—minutes, days, years—they are all yours if you will take them. Wherever you want, however you want. I'll live wherever. I'll die wherever."

Holy fucking shit.

I can't speak. Or move. Or breathe.

"I...I don't understand," I whisper.

"I'm sorry this is happening like this," he goes on. "I'm sorry that I'm professing my love for you in the front seat of your car in a rainy dive bar parking lot. I'm sorry for professing my love for you hours after you were supposed to have dinner with me and my wife. I know this is a lot. And I'm sorry for the selfish way I am laying all this on you. But if I'm being honest with you, Tess, I want to be so selfish with you. I'm tired of living a life that doesn't have you in it."

I just sit there, blinking like an idiot.

He goes on. "I've smiled over the last five years. I've seemingly lived a full life. But the one thing about it is, I'm simply surviving rather than actually living it. I guess, in my head, I've been putting off the living until I can do it with you. I've proven to myself that I *can* live without you. It's just that I don't want to."

It's all the words I have died for him to say.

It's *better* than all the words I've died for him to say.

But his *wife*.

I look up at him, and he knows just what I'm thinking.

"Stevie and me...our time is done," he says. "She doesn't want to be married to someone who is supposed to be with someone else. And I don't want to waste any more time without you."

"So...it's *over?*" I ask him. God damn, this is a lot to process. My mind goes back and forth between wanting to rejoice at the fact that he could be mine and then remembering that he could also be dying.

But either way, I know in my heart that I'll take whatever time there is, and I'll savor every second of it.

He nods.

I don't know what to say.

Sorry your marriage is over because you're in love with me? Sounds weird.

"I...I'm sorry?" I say. A smirk flashes over his lips, and he shakes his head.

"Only you, Tess Connor," he says, "would apologize for someone being in love with you." I can't help but smile back.

"I'm not really sure what I'm supposed to say here," I admit with a shrug. "This is...a lot."

He nods.

"I know, baby girl," he whispers, his hand sliding across the center console to take mine. "I wish it wasn't this way. And I'm sorry that it took me getting a terminal diagnosis to fucking man up and chase you the way I should have five years ago. But hindsight is twenty-twenty, ain't that what they say?"

I smile and nod.

"I want to take you somewhere," he says after a moment of silence. I look up at him and raise an eyebrow. "Overnight. Tomorrow. Will you come?"

I swallow.

A night alone with Cade Waters sounds heavenly.

But his *wife*.

"I want to," I tell him. "But I need to talk to your wife first."

He looks at me and nods.

"You are too good, Tess Connor," he says. "Too good for this Earth and *way* too good for me. But I'm hoping you decide to overlook that." He smiles. "I'll call her. Will you come back to the house tomorrow?"

I nod.

Before he gets out, he turns to face me head on. Then, he leans forward and cups my face in his hands, his lips crashing into mine. I breathe him in, savoring the way he tastes, the way it feels to have his hands on me again. I've learned that letting him love me means letting him leave me, so my body doesn't know how to react to the possibility that this could just be the start for us.

When we finally come apart, he holds his face to mine.

"Tess," he whispers, "this is it. This is our time."

Then, he gets out of my car. But before he shuts the door, he looks down at me.

"You go first." I look at him, puzzled. And he gives

me that devilish smile that I've missed so fucking much. "We both know I'm not letting you drive all the way back to Dalesville in the rain at night by yourself. You go first. I'm right here," he says.

I smile and nod as he closes the door.

This is our time.

God, I hope he's right.

The next evening, I almost can't believe that I am physically pulling back into their driveway after the events of the night before. Love really will make you absolutely fucking batshit crazy.

I draw in a long breath and get out, walking up the porch steps that I ran down like a bat out of hell twenty-four hours ago. When I go to knock on the door, he answers.

"Hi," he says.

"Hi," I say.

He nods his head into the house.

"She didn't stay here last night," he tells me. "She's been inside, packing up some things." I look at him to gauge his reaction. I know him. I know how badly hurting people hurts him. "I'll get her."

"No need," I hear her voice say, and it sends a chill down my spine. "She's right here." She appears behind him in a red sweatshirt and black leggings. I've only ever seen her perfectly put together, but to be honest, she's fucking beautiful in workout clothes, too. She joins us at the door, then holds a hand back out to the porch. "Shall we?" she asks.

I swallow and nod, shooting Cade a look. He looks back at me, but I shake my head, letting him know that I want to talk to Stevie alone.

She leads me back around to the side of the house, back to the chairs we sat in yesterday, where I told her that I'm in love with her husband. But today, she doesn't offer me a drink or a smile. She's just here, existing. She doesn't sit down in a chair. She leans on the railing of the porch and looks at me.

"Cade said you wanted to talk," she says matter-of-factly. I nod. "Go ahead. I'm all ears."

I tuck a piece of hair behind my ear and clear my throat.

"Stevie, I am so sorry—"

"Look, it would be one thing if you swooped in here and tried to steal him from under me," she stops me. "But you didn't Tess. *I* called *you*. *I* asked you to come. You just did what I asked. I don't need—or want—an apology from you. Period."

I pause for a minute. I'm not sure how to go on. I'm not even one hundred percent sure why I needed to talk to her so badly. And after a minute, I think she gets that.

"Look, Tess," she says, "I was blissfully ignorant, up until yesterday, about what it means to really love someone. Or to *be* loved. That man, he would have done anything for me. He *did* do anything for me, including lie to himself for years that I was what he wanted. But he never looked at me the way he looks at you whenever you're near him—the way he even looked at a fucking *picture* of you. And I know things are up in the air. I know everything could come crashing down next week. But I deserve to be looked at like that. To have someone keep a faded photo of me for a decade. And weirdly, you were the one who showed me that. So, I guess, in a weird way, thank you. Whatever happens from here on out, I will never ask about it. I do love that man enough to want him to get to spend whatever time he may have with whomever he wants to spend it with, however he wants to spend it. I just want time, and I want space. This marriage is over, Tess. I won't keep holding onto something that was never really mine."

I nod slowly, but I don't say anything else.

She doesn't want an apology from me. She doesn't want any sort of bullshit about how I feel bad. I think she can tell what kind of person I am. I think she knows that I feel fucking terrible.

But I hope she also knows that I truly want this for her.

The agony of being in love is something everyone should get to experience because, God, it's so fucking beautiful.

I stay out on the porch while she goes inside. After a few minutes, Cade comes back out. He looks at me, and I wait for the other foot to fall. I wait for the crashing and burning that I've been accustomed to waiting for after something goes right for us. Like my brain knows not to get too happy, because it won't last.

That's the thing about Cade and me. I won't

pretend like all the time that we spent together was sunshine and rainbows and mind-blowing sex. I mean, for the short time that we were actually together, there was a *lot* of mind-blowing sex. There were ups, but there were a lot of downs, too. Something waiting around every corner, threatening to pull us apart. Not just threatening, but *actually* pulling us apart. For over a decade.

I like to think of our love like a clear night where the moon lights up the earth, despite the darkness of the sky. Enough to see all the other stars shining through. Enough to know that the sun would come up again.

It may be dark, but Cade is my moon.

He walks toward me and holds out a hand.

"Will you come with me?" he asks. I nod and take his hand, following him down the steps. He walks around to the passenger side of his truck and lets me in. I don't even know where we're going. I don't know how long we will be gone. I don't know how many more days I need to call into work.

And I simply do not care.

Because right now, Cade Waters is mine again.

CHAPTER TWENTY-FOUR

WE DRIVE for about an hour before she finally asks where we're headed. I just smile.

"Somewhere I've told you about a million times but never got to take you."

She thinks for a minute, then her eyes widen.

"Your granddad's cabin?" she asks. I smile and nod. She really doesn't forget *anything*.

About an hour and a half past Dalesville and Grantstown, there's an even smaller town. It's called Youngston, a little valley town in western Maryland. It's where some of the first freed enslaved peoples landed when they moved up north. It's where they put down some roots, worked the land, and made a living for themselves. Somewhere safe.

And it's where my great-great grandfather built a three-room cabin with his own two hands. He passed it down to my grandfather, who passed it to my father, who then passed it to me.

Through the years, we fixed it up, renovated it some, but kept all the character. We didn't want to erase the struggle, everything our ancestors went through to get to this point. It couldn't be more than eight hundred square feet. But every single square foot counted.

I keep this cabin to myself. Grannie and I would come up every so often, back when she could get around easier. My sister and I brought the kids up a time or two, but for the most part, it's just me.

Stevie thought it was cool, but when we came up this way, we traveled a little farther to stay in Meade Lake so that we would be a little more comfortable.

But right now, there's nothing more I want to do than take this girl, my most precious belonging, to my most precious spot.

When we finally pull in, I watch as her eyes widen. She hops out of the truck before I have the chance to get around to her door, and I watch as she walks toward the modest front porch, lips parted, eyes like saucers. When I get to the door with the key, she turns to me.

"This is so cool," she whispers, and I smile. She loves every part of me. That's probably the thing I missed the most when I wasn't with her. Stevie loved me well. She loved the parts she knew of. Even my stubbornness. Even my attitude—when it made its appearance.

But there were parts she couldn't love because she didn't know they existed. With Tess, there's nothing I can hide because she sees it all. She hears what I don't say. She feels what I'm feeling, even if I can't put it into words.

Two bodies, one soul.

When we walk into the house, she looks around and takes it all in. It smells like the wood-burning fireplace that sits in the center of the living room, and the familiar feeling of calm settles over me. I'm in my place, with my person.

I stand quietly and watch her peeking into the tiny bedroom in the back corner, then out to the tiny kitchen. Then, she looks back at me, and I can't help but smile.

"What now?" she whispers. I walk across the room toward her, dropping the duffel bag I packed on the floor. I take her face in my hands and look deep into those big green eyes that have made me weak in the knees for thirteen years. I stroke her cheeks with my thumbs, refamiliarizing myself with every inch of her face. Not rushing it because I'm waiting for her to disappear again. Just slowly savoring it.

"Now," I say, bending down to leave a soft kiss on her right cheek. "Now, we live."

She looks up at me, green eyes full of worry because she knows there might be an expiration date on this, just as there has been every time before. I kiss her right eye, then her left. "Nope," I tell her. "None of that. Not tonight. Right now, we live."

Then, she pushes up on her tiptoes and throws her arms around my neck. Her lips crash into mine, and I can't get over how much I've missed the taste of her. How badly my entire body craves her. I cradle the back of her head in my hand and hook the other under her knee, pulling her up onto me, and I feel her grasp around my neck tighten. She wraps her legs around my waist, and I carry her through the living room into the bedroom. I lay her back gently on the bed, pulling apart only to undress her. I pull her boots off one by one, never breaking eye contact. I gently pull her socks off her feet, then reach for her jeans. In seconds, she's completely naked in front of me, her copper locks splayed out around her like some sort of halo. She reaches up to help me take off my clothes, then pulls me in by the waistband of my gym shorts. She tugs them down, and then I'm naked in front of her, too.

But just before I'm about to descend on her, I see her bottom lip start to tremble.

"Tess?" I whisper, bending down so my arms are on either side of her head. I press my forehead to hers. "What is it, baby?"

"I can't believe this is real," she whispers. "I can't believe all the time we spent apart. And I can't believe I finally have you again."

My heart turns to dust in my chest.

"Oh, sweet girl," I whisper as I tilt her chin up, "for the rest of my days."

I bend down and cover her mouth with mine, pushing myself inside of her. And as we move together, I feel myself falling apart and being put back together at the same time.

This is the best makin' we've ever done.

. . .

We lay in the bed for a few hours, my feet practically hanging over the end of the frame as they always do when I stay here, looking up at the ceiling and talking. She tells me about her friends in Boston, about some of the craziness she's seen on her shifts, about the stillborns she's seen brought to the morgue, about the children who come in, having been abused. I listen to her and stroke her hair, knowing she's never once told anyone else any of this. Knowing that my girl keeps it all to herself because she doesn't feel like anyone can handle it better than she can. Knowing that she recognizes the safe place that she has in me. And thanking the high heavens that I'm here to listen to her again.

We only move when we're hungry, and I go into the kitchen to see what kind of canned meal we can have that hasn't yet expired. When I finish cooking up baked beans and yams, I look at her.

"I should have prepared better," I tell her as I nod to the stove. She laughs.

"This is perfect," she says. "We won't ever forget this meal."

I smile and shake my head.

"We sure won't."

After we eat our "meal," she looks at me.

"I need to get out of these jeans," she says. I shoot her a look and raise my eyebrows up and down. She laughs at me and swats at me. "I'm serious. I didn't know we were staying somewhere and didn't exactly have notice that I needed to pack."

"No worries. I threw extra clothes in my bag so you'd have your pick."

She smiles and leans over the table to kiss me.

"Be right back."

I put the dishes away and make my way to the living room where I sit on the small green-and-red plaid couch that sits adjacent to the fireplace. My grandad's Bible sits on the coffee table, and so do a few other old books that have been passed down.

I pick up *To Kill a Mockingbird* and start flipping through the pages, but I stop after one sentence because she's standing in the doorway of the bedroom in nothing but my green-and-black flannel. It could wrap around her twice, but somehow, she is still completely dazzling in it. My dick stiffens at the mere sight of her, my mouth watering the way it does before you taste something you've been dying for.

"My, my," I whisper as she walks toward me.

"That's my favorite book," she says, slowly taking it out of my hands. She pulls the fabric up above her knees and straddles me on the couch. I slide my hands up to her hips as she bends down to kiss me, her tongue tracing mine, her teeth grazing my bottom lip.

"Mine, too," I whisper back. She starts moving slowly back and forth on my lap, and I feel how warm her center is through my shorts.

"Cade," she whispers into my ear as she kisses my jaw and nibbles on my lobe.

"Yeah, baby," I answer.

"It's been almost ten years," she says. "We're overdue for some breakin'."

I smile as she sucks on my neck, sending chills up all over my body.

"Oh, yeah?" I ask her. She nods slowly.

"Mm-hmm," she says. Then, she positions her lips directly next to my ear again. "You got some new moves for me?"

I slide one hand around to cup her ass and slip my other up her front until they're circling her pussy.

"Oh, little one…" I grin. "You have no idea."

I let my fingers play with her, stroke her, slide through her wetness, while my other hand reaches up to unbutton the shirt. God, everything about her is so fucking beautiful. Her skin is so soft and creamy, her scent is intoxicating. I can see the tattoo I got her peeking out from inside the shirt, and I freeze for a minute. I remember the night I took her to get it. Hours spent next to her while Thad did his work. A beautiful, detailed moonlit scene, with the silhouettes of trees up and down her rib cage. I stop before I get to the last buttons, and she gives me a curious look. I lean forward so that I'm centimeters from her lips.

"I kinda want to fuck you while you have my shirt on," I whisper, and the faintest smile flashes across her lips as she lets her head drop back while my fingers continue their exploring. But just as I'm about to flip her over and fill her up with myself, she slides just out of my reach. She puts her hands on my shoulders and pushes me back against the couch, then slides off my lap and onto the floor. She tugs on my waistband, and my mind goes haywire at the thought of what's about to happen.

"You're gonna have to wait," she tells me as she pulls down my pants and boxers and grabs my throbbing dick. She slides her hands up and down painfully slow, her eyes widening at the sight of me. There's something so carnal about seeing her hot for me and watching her lick her lips just before she takes me into her mouth. She starts with just the tip, swirling her tongue around till I know she's already had a taste. I drop my head back as she takes more of me in, moving her mouth up and down my shaft as her hands still grip me. She tucks a hand under my sack and rubs it, gently squeezing in rhythm with her mouth. It drives me fucking wild, and I reach my hand out to stroke her hair as she slurps and sucks and gags on my length. I reach down when I feel myself getting close and pull her to her feet.

"Okay, little one," I say, "enough of that before you make me come all over you."

She smirks and wipes her mouth.

"That's kind of the goal," she says.

"Oh, don't you worry," I tell her as I stand up. "There will be plenty of time for that."

I pull her to her feet and turn us around so that she's backed up to the couch and take a step closer to her. "Now, take a seat." She looks down at the couch next to her, then back up to me with a smirk. And I know what she's doing. She's challenging me. She wants me to take charge.

So, I do. I step closer to her and slide my hand down between her legs. I dip two fingers inside of her and move them from side to side while she bites her lip and moans.

"Take. A. Seat," I command. And this time, she

does. I step closer. "Now, lie back." She does. I tap both of her knees. "Open."

She looks up at me and bites her lip, and it sends me into overdrive. I'm usually in pretty good command in the bedroom, but something about this girl makes me want to turn into a horny fucking teenager. Slowly, she lets her knees drop, giving me the perfect view of that perfect pussy. I crawl up the couch and bring my lips just inches from it before I look up at her, making eye contact.

"Good girl," I tell her, and she drops her head back, clutching the sides of the couch in preparation for what's to come. Then, I dive in, starting to devour her. I kiss her lips first, then trace them with my tongue, up and down and in between. I suck her clit into my mouth gently as I slide my hands up under the fabric of my shirt. One hand circles her breast and tugs on her nipple, while the other pushes gently against the low part of her stomach. I feel her start to clench, and I know she's close. She reaches down to push my head into her deeper, and I smile, the sweet scent of her making me fucking crazy.

"Cade, I'm gonna…"

"Do it, baby," I tell her as I continue to fuck her with my tongue. "Do it, right here. Cover me."

And then her legs straighten on my shoulders, shaking as they fall limp over me. I get one last taste before I scoot back. She's panting on the couch, one arm draped over her eyes. I smile at her as she peeks at me.

"I forgot how fucking good you are at that," she says. I smile and shrug.

"We all have our talents," I tell her. She pushes up on her elbows, then sits up. She pushes me back onto the couch again so that I'm sitting back, and she straddles me once again.

"What do you think you're doing?" I ask her.

"I'm gonna fuck you while I wear your shirt," she says with a smirk. Then, before I have a moment for a witty reply, she reaches down to grab hold of me, positioning me under her, and slides down onto me, taking me all the way in.

We both gasp simultaneously, and I grip her hips while she moves back and forth, making me fit inside her. Then, she starts bouncing, and I fucking lose it.

"Oh, my God," I moan as she moves, my shirt sliding off her shoulders, her hair falling out of the bun on the top of her head. I squeeze her ass as she pants on top of me. "Take it all, little one."

She slides a hand up and clutches her own breast, the other digging into my shoulder as she moves faster and faster.

"Oh, fuck, baby," I moan out, "that pussy is so good."

She leans forward and puts her lips to my ear.

"It's yours, Cade," she tells me. "All yours."

I growl at the thought of it. At the pleasure of having her all to myself, finally. And at the mere thought of her—any part of her—ever being anyone else's. I'm aware how ridiculous it sounds, being that I am the one who is still legally married. But it's all I can think about when I lay eyes on her.

Mine.

I push myself up and lift her gently so that I slip out of her, her juices all over my lap. I grab her by the waist and flip her over so that she's facing away from me. I pull her back onto my lap and push myself back into her, making her gasp again as I do.

"Oh, God," she cries out. She clutches onto my thighs as her head drops back to my shoulder, and I wrap my fingers around her neck as I pull her face to mine. I devour her lips as I slide my other hand down to her clit, my fingers sliding around in circles. She's fucking soaked, and so is the couch. But I don't fucking care. I'd do this in the middle of a fucking park with her.

But just as her body starts to stiffen, she pauses.

"Wait, wait," she says, and I freeze. She turns to me. "Fuck me from behind."

I swear my eyes roll back in my head. I push us up and turn us so that she's on all fours on the couch in front of me. I grip her hips and gently push her head down toward the cushion before I plow into her. She's so tight, the grip so intense that I almost blow the first time I enter. But not yet. Not till I know she's coming with me.

I reach around again until I find it, pressing two fingers in a circle on her bud as I fuck her from behind. The sight of her little body taking me in is almost more than I can bear. But I refuse to come before she does. And if I do, she won't know until she does the same.

I hear her breath quickening beneath me, and I see her slide her arms out in front of her, grabbing onto the arm of the couch.

"Oh," she moans. "Oh, my God. Please. Yes…" I rub faster as I fuck, sweat trickling down the side of my face. "Cade…oh, oh…." And then she goes rigid. I unleash myself, letting myself go and coming inside her with such force that it shakes my whole body. I moan as I let myself sink down on top of her. We lie like that for a few minutes, me tracing circles on her shoulder that my shirt has slipped off of again, her drawing in long, slow breaths. Finally, I push up as I leave a kiss on her shoulder.

"Come on, baby," I tell her, holding out my hand. "Let's get cleaned up and go to bed."

She moans as she rolls to her back, her eyes closed.

"I can't," she says with a smile. "You used up all my energy."

I laugh as I bend down and scoop her up with absolutely no effort whatsoever.

"Not a problem."

I carry her to the bathroom and set her down while I turn on the shower. I reach over and unbutton the last few buttons of my shirt, then take it off. And when I do, I see the trail of wetness between her legs, and I lick my lips. There's something really fucking sexy about seeing myself dripping out of her.

Mine.

I turn the water on to just under scalding hot, then lead her into the tiny shower that we barely fit in together. I turn her around, squirt some shampoo in my hands, and start to wash her hair. Her eyes are closed as she lets me bathe her, and I have this over-whelming feeling to hold her. I love this. I love *doing* for her. Anything. Fucking her silly so she doesn't know which way is up. Carrying her across the room. Holding her when she needs me. Taking her to get a tattoo. Giving her a ride home. It doesn't matter what it is. I just want her to be able to shut her brain off with me. I want to be her respite. I watched for years as she became an adult too quickly, as she took on roles she had no business taking on, as she became the caretaker of her father, the woman of the house before she was a woman herself.

And I watched as her father let her, not out of mali-cious intent, but out of ignorance. Out of not knowing how to help.

But I *do* know how to help.

We finish up in the shower, and I turn the water off. We dry off, she puts on a t-shirt of mine, me in my boxers, and we climb into bed.

A few hours later, I stir when my arm goes completely numb. She's fast asleep with it tucked under her head, but I don't dare move her. As far as I'm concerned, it could fall off. I just want her comfortable. Content.

I roll to my side as I stare at her, the perfect lines of her face, the long lashes that fan the tops of her cheeks while she breathes. And for the first time tonight, the thought enters my mind...that this could all end soon. Again. I could leave her behind.

I know there could never be enough time for me to show her how much she means to me, terminal illness or no terminal illness.

But I'd sure love the opportunity to try.

CHAPTER TWENTY-FIVE

tess

WHEN I FIRST OPEN MY eyes, I can't believe he's really here. I can't believe the events of the last forty-eight hours all actually happened. That we're here, together, in this bed. That I can feel his heart beating through the stillness of the morning. That I can reach out and touch the freckle on the bridge of his nose and the small patch of them under his eye. That I can trace his beard, and his lips, and smell his skin. I can watch his tattoos gently move up and down with every peaceful breath he takes.

He's real, and he's right here in front of me.

After a lifetime, it's finally *our* time.

I have no idea how long I lay here watching him, but I know the sun is finally peeking through the small window behind the bed. Slowly, I watch his eyelashes fan against his cheeks as he peels his eyes open and looks at me.

"Damn," he whispers.

"What?"

He shakes his head.

"I could literally be dying, and seeing you like this, first thing in the morning, makes everything else go away."

I swallow.

Literally dying.

I smile as I reach a hand up to trace his bottom lip.

"I dreamt about us last night," I tell him. He cocks an eyebrow.

"Oh yeah?" he says, raising them up and down. I laugh and shake my head.

"Not *that* kind of dream," I say. "Although, I have had plenty of those kinds of dreams about you in my life."

He leans back, feigning surprise.

"Okay, we are gonna circle back to that," he says, waving his finger in a circular motion. "But go on. Tell me."

I laugh and push up onto my elbow, resting my head in my hand.

"We were just sitting in your truck," I say. "The old one. The OG pickup."

He laughs.

"You mean the rusty old hunk of junk that was held together with duct tape and a prayer?" he chuckles. I smile. He drives a bigger, sleeker, newer truck than the one he used to drive me around in. But I liked the old one. I'm sentimental like that.

"Hey," I say. "I *loved* that truck. Some very, *very* good things happened in that truck."

He laughs and shakes his head again.

"Okay, okay. Go on. What happened in my truck?"

I look at him and smile.

"Basically nothing," I tell him. He cocks his head again and lifts an eyebrow.

"Nothing? Not even a quick kiss or a boob graze?"

I laugh again. It feels so good to laugh with him.

"Not even a boob graze. We were sitting there, quiet, listening to some music, just looking at each other."

He smiles at me and reaches a finger out to tuck my hair behind my ear.

"That sounds like an amazing dream," he whispers as he leans forward to kiss me. Even kissing him is so natural, almost involuntary, like our bodies just know when they need a taste of the other.

When we come apart, he lifts his eyes to me. That honey glow about them is dissipating, and it feels like they are darker than usual.

"We have to go soon, don't we?" I ask him. He nods slowly, his eyes tracing every corner of my face. I push him onto his back and crawl over to him, straddling him on my knees. I let the sheets fall and look down at him. "Okay. But first we got some makin' to do."

An hour or so later, we're cleaning up the cabin, throwing his clothes back into his bag, and locking the front door. We walk down the porch steps hand in hand, and he stops for a moment. He turns back to me and lets go of my hand, then takes a few steps back into the yard.

"What are you doing?"

He smiles.

"Just taking a mental picture of my favorite human in my favorite place," he says. I smile and nervously tuck my hair behind my ear. It's still so surreal. And even with him, I never get used to compliments. And he knows it. He pulls me in for a long kiss, and then we walk to his truck. He opens my door, then his, and we drive off into the direction of the town that made us, us.

As we get onto the highway, he reaches for my leg, tucking his fingers under my thigh and holding on with a grip that makes me feel both safe and incredibly horny. Funny how that happens when you're where you're supposed to be. It feels territorial, and I really, *really* like that I'm his.

"I gotta tell you something," he says, snapping me out of my almost-drooling state.

"Hmm?"

"Stevie wants to be around for whatever happens with the doctor and whatever treatment I decide on," he says. I swallow. There's a weight on my chest, but I nod.

"And is that what you want?" I ask.

"You know me," he says with a shrug. I smile.

"Yeah," I say. "I do. And I know you never want to upset anyone."

He smiles.

"Not really my thing," he says. "Although, I've done a pretty good job of it, with just about everyone in my life."

I shake my head.

"Stop," I tell him. "Answer me."

"I mean…" he starts. He pauses for a minute and stares out the windshield. "She and I have been through a lot together. I think it makes sense. Yeah, she should be there."

I nod.

"I agree," I tell him. "Honestly."

He nods and squeezes my leg.

There's another long pause, and then I ask him the question I've been dying to ask him since I came back to Dalesville.

"How are you feeling about all of this? Have you made a decision?" I ask him.

He looks at me, and his lips pull up into a smirk.

"How long you been waitin' to ask me that?" he asks. I lean over and playfully push his shoulder.

"*So* fucking long," I tell him as we both laugh. "It's been tough, but I didn't want to be one more person asking you all the tough questions."

He looks at me.

"That's because you know me better than anyone on this planet," he whispers. "Even after all this time. You know when I need someone to ask, you know when I need someone to listen, and you know when I need someone to just shut up and be there."

The look in his eyes is heavy as they move from me, to the road, to me. But then he smiles.

"You also seem to know when I just need you to get naked and on top of me, and that is working out phenomenally," he says. We both laugh again, and I squeeze his hand.

"I'm so glad I could be of service," I finally say. He lifts my hand to his lips and presses a kiss to it. Then, his eyes grow dark again.

"I think I'm gonna do it," he says. "The treatment. All of it."

I swallow.

I'm not a specialist in melanoma, or cancer in general, but I have enough medical knowledge and enough oncology friends from the hospital to know that if he's stage three, the cancer has already spread. And if he doesn't move fast on some sort of treatment, then he might run out of time to even make a decision. Having the spot and his lymph nodes removed will help his doctors tell what the damage is. What his best treatment options are. How long he might truly have left.

How long *we* might have left.

I squeeze his hand.

"Then surgery is what we will do," I say. He lifts his eyes to me again.

"'We?'" he says with a smile.

"We," I tell him. "In this life, and in the next."

We stop at Aunt Rie's first so I can shower quickly and change into new clothes. Then, we jump back in the truck and head to his house. When we pull up into his driveway, Stevie's car is parked. We have about a half-hour before we need to leave for his appointment with his oncologist. I swallow. Before the *three* of us need to leave for his oncologist. God, this is weird.

He tells me he wants to grab a quick shower, too, and looks at me like he's not sure what to say.

"I'll be fine," I tell him with a smile. "I can wait outside."

"Don't be silly," I hear her voice say from the kitchen as she makes her way to us. "I just made a pot of coffee. Have a cup while he gets ready."

He looks to her, then looks to me. I nod so he knows we will be fine, even if I'm not quite sure that's the truth. He leaves reluctantly, and I follow her into the kitchen. She hands me a mug from the cabinet next to the sink and motions to the fridge.

"Cream?" she asks.

"Oh, sure," I tell her. She opens the fridge and takes it out, handing it to me.

"Have a seat," she says, motioning to the table. So, I do. I'm not here to cause more disruption. Despite the fact that this woman was living out the life I had dreamt about with the man I dreamt of it with, I have nothing against her.

There's a long silence, and I look at her.

"Stevie, I don't have to go to the appointment today," I tell her. I swallow back my guilt at not being there for him. But looking at this woman's face, I feel myself being torn apart.

"Does he want you to be there?" she asks. I nod slowly. "Then, that's exactly where you should be."

Another long, uncomfortable silence.

"I just have to say," I tell her candidly, "you have to be the most mature, gracious, selfless person I have ever met in my entire life."

She sips her coffee and sets her mug down. Then, she actually breaks into a smile. Then, she starts to giggle. Then, she starts to laugh. And not just a meek, quiet little laugh. A loud, booming, hearty, belly laugh.

And then I start laughing. And I can't stop.

Tears are rolling down both of our cheeks, and finally, she looks over at me as we both catch our breath.

"Did you also just realize how absolutely absurd this all is?" she asks through giggles. I laugh and nod my head.

"Fucking insane," I tell her as I clutch my stomach.

She lets out a long sigh as she finally gets herself together. She looks out the window for a minute, then her eyes find me. I swallow.

"Can I ask you a question?" I ask. She nods. "Why did you call me? I mean, you could have just let it go—let me go—and carried on. It could have just been you two."

Her eyes drop down to her mug as she spins it around on the table in front of her.

"A woman's instinct is never wrong," she says with a sad smile. "And I guess I felt like, if he was going to live, I didn't want to live the rest of our lives not knowing for sure if he wanted me the way I wanted him. And if he was going to die, I couldn't bear to keep him from the one person he truly loved." Her voice cracks as she speaks, and I feel my own jaw trembling.

"You know," she goes on, "I'm not sure if it's just because everything is on hyper-drive right now because we have no idea how much time he has. So, maybe this will all change in a few months' time. But I don't feel *angry*. I mean, I feel betrayed, sure. But not because he loves you. I don't mean to say that he never loved me, because I know that he did. Or does. I mean, he tried to make himself be *in* love with me. But he can't be. Because he never fell out of love with you."

"I...I'm sorry, Stevie. I—"

"I meant it when I said that I don't need an apology from you. The truth is, all you did was exist. But from this day on, if I'm going to be with someone, I want him to look at me the way my husband looks at you. I deserve it."

I nod.

Jesus. She deserves a fucking king.

"That man in there...he really is a good husband. He's my best friend. But best friends aren't always soulmates."

A moment later, we hear the bedroom door open, and Cade pads down the hall. He looks at us, back and forth, a puzzled look on his face. He knows something is up, but he's not sure what it is.

"You ladies ready?" he asks. She looks at me, and I look at her. We both nod. He thinks we're nodding because we're ready. But we both know that we're nodding because now we're bonded. We both love the same man, and though it's different, one love doesn't negate the other. And as I look at the man who has had my heart since the day I met him, I know I have her to thank. Because he hasn't changed all that much. He still smiles. He still lights up the room. She may not have been the piece that fit his, but she did make him happy. And every night, when I left my mark on the moon, and I hoped and prayed that he was somewhere else smiling, he was. And it was because of Stevie.

CHAPTER TWENTY-SIX

WE'RE SITTING in the exam room, and I'm on the table, kicking my legs like a child. I'm in a sexy hospital gown, looking back and forth from the woman I married to the woman who changed my whole world.

It's a strange juxtaposition to have them here like this. It might be a cold, sterile setting, but they're both with me. And I'm not sure how else to describe it, except that it's almost like reading a book about my own life. Stevie was a chapter—a very important chapter—and she's part of the reason I am who I am. There were walls I never took down for Stevie, but despite that, she gave me stability. She gave me a home. She taught me how to work as a team. She loved me.

And with Tess, it's like she's who the whole damn story is about. And the crazy thing is, with Stevie, things were easier. They were mellow, calm. Tess was a storm. She still is. Our love is a storm. But we've only ever gotten to experience our love to the fullest when we knew we were going to lose it.

And here we are again.

None of us say anything. Stevie is reading a brochure on melanoma from cover to cover. Tess is looking at me. She looks poised, calm, collected. Her eyes are narrowed on mine, and I know it's because she's reading me. She's watching the way I move. My body language. My knuckles turning white from clutching the table. She absorbs my energy just like I do to hers. No walls with her. Because even if I put them up, she'd tear right through them.

"Hey," she says, and I look at her. "I'm right here."

I feel Stevie's eyes on us, but before anyone can say anything, there's a knock on the door, and Dr. Sang walks in.

"How we doin', folks?" he asks. He's a tall, strong, Asian man with a sleeve tattoo that shows through the white fabric of his lab coat. I'm pretty sure he's younger than I am, and he's funny. That's why I chose him. I felt like if someone was going to tell you you're going to die, it's better that they can at least make you smile.

He leans forward and shakes my hand, then nods to Stevie. He looks at Tess and pauses like he's waiting for an introduction, but after some contemplation, the three of us decide against it. Not real sure how to say, "This is my wife, and this is my soulmate," without saying those exact words and having someone stare at us like we're all nuts—even though we just might be.

"Hey, Doc," I say with a smile. "I got pretty for you today." I hold up the gown, and he laughs and shakes his head.

"I appreciate that," he says. "You're the best-looking patient I've had all day. But don't tell the others." He pats the end of the exam table. "Let's get that leg up here so I can take a look."

I do as I'm told, swiveling around to put my leg straight up on the table. He pushes my gown up a bit with a gloved hand and repositions the lamp that's at the end of the table so he can get a better look. He uses some sort of tool to measure the spot on my leg again, then rolls over to the counter behind him to write something down on my chart.

"Have you given any thought to our last conversation?" he asks as he rolls his stool closer to the table.

I swallow, then look at both of them sitting in the chairs across the room. I nod.

"I'd like to move forward with all of it. All the treatment options we discussed," I tell him. He looks relieved as he nods.

"I am very happy to hear that. Just because it's stage three doesn't mean it's hopeless, by any means. The quicker we get in and remove the spot and the lymph nodes and start radiation, the better. I'll have one of our cancer nurse navigators come back in to get you scheduled and go through the details. Do you have any questions for me?"

I swallow and shake my head.

"I think that's all, Doc," I say. I don't really want to do this. But I *do* want to live. So, here we are. He shakes my hand again, then turns to Stevie.

"Mrs. Waters, can I answer any questions for you?"

There's an awkward silence as Stevie freezes for a moment. I nervously look at Tess.

Mrs. Waters.

That's the name I should have given to her. But just as the thought enters my mind, I think about what she said.

I'm not really interested in being anything other than a Connor, anyway.

I almost smile to myself. That's fine. I don't care if she changes her name to Princess Consuela Banana Hammock, just like Phoebe on *Friends*.

I'll call her by any name she chooses, as long as I can also call her *mine*.

That juxtaposition again.

She clears her throat.

"Um, yes, actually," she says. "What will the recovery be like for him, post-surgery? Anything special we'll need to do for him?"

I swallow again as I listen to them go back and forth, my eyes locked on Tess. Then, Stevie turns to her.

"Did you have any questions?" she asks Tess. I stare at them both with wide eyes. Tess thinks about it for a moment, then shakes her head.

"I think you've both about covered it," she says. Then, she looks right at Stevie. "I'll be here for whatever you need."

~

T.D. COLBERT

Two hours later, I'm changing into a hoodie and shorts and walking back out into my living room. My wife and the love of my life sit next to each other on the couch, mugs of decaf coffee in hand. They turn to me and quiet down as I enter the room, and I feel like I'm supposed to be giving a speech or something.

"Hi," I say.

They both smile.

"Sit down," Stevie says, motioning to the chair adjacent to them.

I give them both a curious look, but then do as I'm told.

"We've been talking about the surgery," Stevie starts. She looks to Tess. I feel my heart rate increase.

"I'm going to go back to Boston tomorrow," she says, and I feel my heart sink to the floor. "I'm going to request an extended leave of absence and then be back in two weeks when you have surgery. I'll stay here in the house with you while you recover."

Thank God. I don't want her to have to take care of me, but I also don't want her to leave—ever again. I know it sounds dramatic, but we've done our time apart. We've done our waiting. No more. Not for as long as I live.

Then, she looks to Stevie.

"I'm going to pack up my necessities and go to stay with Della for a while." I narrow my eyes on her. I don't know exactly how I was expecting this to play out, but this feels wrong.

I stop her.

"Steve, I can go," I tell her. "I don't mind, really. We can go to the cabin. You can have the house."

She shakes her head.

"The cabin is too far away from your doctors and the hospital, if anything were to go wrong. And besides that…" she says, pausing to look down at her hands. She draws in a breath and looks back at me. I know this face. It's the *I-will-not-cry* face. The face she makes right before she does, in fact, cry. "This house doesn't mean the same anymore. I don't *want* to stay here."

I nod slowly.

"I get it," I tell her, a pang of guilt hitting me in the chest. I hate hurting people.

"Della is ready for me," she tells me. "Got the guest room all set up while I look for something else."

Della is Stevie's longtime friend that lives here in Dalesville. She and her little boy have a house not far from the center of town. I know Della will keep things quiet. Not that I give a rat's ass what anyone thinks of me. Never really have. But I do care about Stevie. I don't want to create a mess for her to deal with. Questions for her to have to answer long after I'm gone.

Stevie looks back to Tess.

"After surgery, we will both be here. I'll see how you're doing before and will make sure you have everything you need." Then, she looks at Tess. "Both of you."

They nod at each other, and I feel like there is some sort of strange sisterhood.

Both of these women love me.

I'm one lucky son of a bitch.

· · ·

After a little more conversation, Stevie goes to the bedroom to pack up both of her extra-large suitcases. We help her get them to the car, and then we wave goodbye. Then, I walk back inside with Tess and close the door behind us. Then, I just stare at her.

"Is this real?" I ask her. She tilts her head to the side.

"Is what real?" she says.

"You. Me. This," I say, motioning between us. She smiles as she crosses the floor toward me, pushing up onto her tiptoes. She wraps her arms around my neck and pulls me in for a long kiss.

"Don't think it gets more real than this, Waters," she says before she kisses me again. We stand there for a moment, holding each other, our eyes closed, our breaths syncing up.

"You know what's funny?" she whispers, our heads pressed together as we sway back and forth slowly.

"What's that?"

"I had this thought the whole way down here," she says. "Well, more of a fear, really."

"Fear of what?"

"That it might not have been real," she goes on. I pull back and look at her.

"What does that mean?" I ask. She shrugs.

"I don't know. I guess I just worried that maybe I made it all up. How we felt about each other. Or even... if you felt it then, that you might not have felt it now. I thought about Lauren, Stevie, whoever Rain Girl was."

She pauses, and I laugh.

"'Rain Girl,'" I say, and shake my head. "Do you

forget *anything?*"

"I wondered if I would just become like them. A memory. Maybe even a painful one. But one that you would eventually move past. I wondered if maybe you would end up happier without me."

I stand back and her hold her off of me, staring down into those emerald-green eyes. Eyes that are glassy now.

"Tessa Lynn Connor," I say," Once you feel this, you don't *stop* feeling it." She nods and blinks, the tears spilling from her eyes. I wipe them with my thumbs and cup her face in my hands. "There is no moving past you. You're it for me, baby girl. In this life and every life. I'll find you again."

She nods and pushes herself up again, her lips crashing into mine. I reach down and hook my hand under the backs of her knees, hoisting her up so she can wrap her legs around my waist. She clenches them tight around my waist, her lips on mine, then on my ear, then on my neck. I feel her grind her center against mine, and I walk us toward the living room. But she stops me.

"Not in here," she whispers. I pull back, confused. "I'm not gonna fuck you in the house you bought with your wife."

I stand still for a moment, unsure what to do next.

Then, she bites my neck gently and looks up at me.

"Take me up to the woods." I set her down on the ground and take her hand. I grab the throw blanket off the back of the couch, and we walk out the front door. I want to run to my spot. Fucking sprint there, actually.

But I'm going to take my time and savor every single second with her. Finally,, though, we get to the small clearing in the woods where my boulder sits. I throw the blanket on top of it, folding it twice so that it's as soft as possible for her. Then, I tug on her hand, swinging her around in front of me.

She smiles as I lift her up onto the boulder. I kiss her lips, her jaw, her cheeks, her neck. I slide my hand down to unbutton her jeans, and I use my other hand to lay her back gently against the blanket. I tug my own shorts and boxers down and let myself spring free. As I lean over top of her, she puts a hand to my chest.

"Wait," she says. Then, her eyes move up. "Look around us."

And I do. The leaves are all different colors, the air has a chill to it that's enough to let you know summer's over, and there's no sound except the wind blowing through the trees. A big blue sky hangs above us, and I draw in a long breath. Then, I look down at her.

"This has to be almost as good as the time in the rain, right?" she says. I laugh and hang my head.

"Do you forget *anything?*" I ask her. She smiles and shakes her head.

"I know one thing," she whispers, reaching her hands up to pull me down to her. "I won't be forgetting *this.*"

Her tongue finds mine, and now I'm as hard as the fucking rock she's lying on. She slides a hand down to grip me, moving it up and down on my shaft. I stand back and lick my fingers, then move them in a slow circular motion around her clit.

She moans and bites her lip, her hips bucking just the slightest.

"You want this, baby girl?" I ask her. She nods.

"Yes, please," she says.

"You gonna be a good girl and take this for me?"

She nods again.

"You gonna let me fuck you out here in the open?"

She nods again.

"Yes, sir."

"Good girl."

And then, I do. I feel her wetness on my hands, and I lick my fingers just before I tug her jeans down a little more. I push into her, holding her arms above her head, and she lets out a scream of pleasure.

"Oh, fuck," she cries. She's so fucking tiny, this little girl. But she's proven time and time again that she can handle all of me, and it's *so* fucking sexy. I grab the backs of her legs and push them up toward her stomach. She's wide open, taking me stroke after stroke like a fucking champ.

I pull out of her slowly, my dick slick with her juices, and tap her ass.

"Flip over," I tell her. She's on her knees now, and I tug her ass toward me. As I push back into her, I look up at the sky again. There's something about fucking her out here that's making me primal. I quicken the pace, pushing harder and harder into her with every single thrust. She's clutching onto the blanket, but every time I move to ask if she's okay, she begs for more.

When I feel like I'm about to blow, I turn her back over again, laying her back down gently. She looks up at me, her eyes big and full of wonder for what I have next for her. And as badly as I want to continue fucking her silly out here in these woods, something in me switches gears. Now, I want nothing more than to stare into her eyes while I make her come. I want to be the last thing she sees before she sees stars.

I push back into her slowly, gripping the back of her thigh with one hand and the back of her head with the other. I hold her head still so I can look at her, and she knows what's happening. She's moaning and biting her lip, but her eyes are filling with tears. This breakin' just turned into makin'.

And just as her eyes roll back in her head, her legs stiffening on either side of me, I come inside of her, too. And as we both lie there, panting, bodies slick with each other's sweat, I decide that she's the last thing I want to see before I go altogether.

One look at Tess before all I see is black.

CHAPTER TWENTY-SEVEN

tess

I'M ABOUT three-quarters of the way to Boston now, my little Toyota cruising up I-95. There hasn't been a whole lot of traffic yet, even going through New York, which is a bit strange. I haven't told Annie and Alexa I'm coming back. I plan to just be there when they get back. I have no idea how to explain this story to anyone, even my two best friends.

I don't know how to explain that I've finally ended up with the love of my life. And also that he's technically married. And also that he might be dying. The last few days in Dalesville have been a whirlwind, but the plus is that everything has happened in our own little world. The only people who really know what is going on are me, Cade, Stevie, and Aunt Rie. And I guess, now, Stevie's friend, Della.

But whether we are ready for it or not, time is still moving. And for Cade and I, time might be running out.

It's strange, because a few months ago—even a few

days ago—I would have told you I was happy, content. My life revolved completely around my job. I didn't even eat or pee unless I had enough time between patients. But now, it seems like such a small thing.

Don't get me wrong, I love nursing. It's heartbreaking and tears you apart, but every once in a while, you get a patient that changes the way you see the whole world or the way you see yourself. And to know that you were the one with them during their darkest hours, and you were the one who pulled them through...*that's* what makes all the heartbreak worth it.

I don't want to stop nursing. But I do want to leave Boston. I want to go back home. I want to be home with him. Somewhere along the way, I know I'll find my way back to it. I'm just hoping like hell he will be with me when I do.

After another two hours, I pull into a spot on the street across from our apartment building, grab my stuff, and walk through the door. I make my way up to our fourth-floor walk-up and pull my keys out of my bag. I take in a long breath. This might be the last time I put this key in this door for a long time.

This apartment is special to me.

It was the place that taught me that I could be alone. I could take care of myself. I could be my own shoulder to lean on.

But it was in Dalesville—or wherever he was, really—that I learned I didn't have to do all those things. I could let my guard down. I could unclench my jaw and take a breath, knowing that someone else was going to carry the heavy stuff whenever I felt tired—or even when I didn't know I was feeling tired. Just because he loved me enough to want to.

I walk in the door and flick the entryway lights on, but to my surprise, the living room television is on with an episode of *Schitt's Creek* playing. On one couch lies a drowsy but conscious Alexa, and on the other lies a snoring Annie.

"Whoa!" Alexa says. "What are you doing here? Do we know you, stranger?"

Annie pushes up slowly and rubs at her eyes, blinking and readjusting her crooked glasses. She looks at Alexa, then over to me, and her eyes widen.

They both smile as I stand there, and at first, I smile back. I love them so much. And not being with them for a while—or maybe, if I even let myself think it, forever—will be an adjustment. It's so rare that all three of us are in this apartment together at the same time. Tonight is one of those nights. And it just happens to be a night when I need it the most. I just stand there, right by the front door, bag in hand, keys in the other, staring at them.

"Hello? Did you go back home and forget how to speak?" Annie says. Her and Alexa chuckle at first, but then they notice the expression on my face. They both stand in unison and start to walk toward me as my jaw starts to tremble. "Shit, dude," Annie says as she wraps her arms around me. Then, Alexa does the same, wrapping her arms around us both. And we just stand there for a moment until I can collect myself, the tears streaming off my cheeks. After a few minutes, they walk me into the apartment. Annie takes my keys, Alexa takes my bag, and we all sit on the couch together. Annie runs back to the kitchen for a minute, and I hear her popping the cork on a fresh bottle of wine. In a flash, she's back with three filled-to-the-brim glasses.

"Okay," she says. "Now we're ready."

"Yeah," Alexa says. "Hit us."

I draw in a long breath, followed by a long sip of the wine. It's drier than I typically like, but I don't care.

I sit cross-legged between them, each of them turned to face me. Then, I start to talk. And I tell them *everything,* starting from the very beginning.

When I first met him. How he was the one who was with me when my dad died. How he beat up the bouncer that night in the bar. How we were together once, but it was over in the blink of an eye.

The tears well as I tell them how I've never felt the way I feel about him for anyone else, including Elijah. How I'd thrown myself into my job because I didn't want to ever be still. Because when things got too quiet, that's when my heart would wander back to him.

I tell them about how his wife called. And about the cancer. And about how over the last three days, we realized that we were never going to be whole without each other. And how his wife was the one who brought us together. And how she was the one to end their marriage.

They both just listen intently, nodding every so often, rubbing my hands. I see their eyes turn to saucers every so often when I get to the juicy parts.

I tell them how he's having the surgery next week.

And about how I'll be taking leave and heading back home for an open-ended amount of time.

"So, basically, I went home and ended up with the absolute love of my life. But the catch is, he could be dying."

Then, we're all quiet for a minute. I slow down my breathing and swipe the last of the tears from my cheeks. Wow, it felt good to get that all out. I hadn't realized how much weight I was carrying until I let it go.

"Well, damn, gal," Annie says. "That's...a fuckin' *lot*."

"Yeah, what she said," Alexa says, squeezing my hand. "I don't know how you've held it together this long."

I smile and nod.

"It's been a crazy couple of days."

"You know," Annie says. "I feel bad for the wife. What's her name? Rickie?"

I chuckle and shake my head.

"Stevie," I correct her.

"Right, yeah. Stevie. I mean, that's gotta be tough. But what she said to you, it's kinda true. She is the one who brought you back to him, and it's probably because she knew all along that you two were sort of inevitable."

"It's true," Alexa says. "Women can always tell, ya know? And she probably always knew, on some level, that he was never really hers."

I nod.

"That's what she said, actually," I say. "But I still wish it didn't happen the way it did."

"I know," Alexa says. "But think about it this way. Now, she has the chance to find someone amazing. The person she's really supposed to be with."

"Yeah," Annie says. "And let's be honest, that chick deserves someone who worships her every fucking move, and gives her mind-blowing orgasms, and gives her back rubs."

We all chuckle.

"I hope she finds that," I say. "I really do."

"For a minute, let's pretend this whole cancer thing isn't part of the equation, okay?" Annie says. I nod. "You have been through a *lot*, Tess. A lot. Dude, I don't know anyone else who has had as much loss as you have. So, hear me when I tell you this, okay?"

I nod again.

"You *deserve* this. You deserve him."

I swallow. Alexa takes my hand again.

"You do, Tess," she says. "I know the way you found each other again isn't exactly orthodox, but there's a *reason* you found each other again. Even if..." Her voice trails off.

"Even if he dies," I finish for her, and she nods solemnly.

"Yeah. Even then," she goes on, "would it have been worth it for just one more day with him?"

I think about her question for a minute, and I nod.

"It would have been worth it for one more minute with him."

They both smile at me.

"Then, there ya go," Alexa says.

"So, now," Annie says, taking a bite of her tortilla chip that's drowning in guacamole, "is he good in bed?"

I laugh out loud, and it feels so good.

"You have *no* idea," I tell them.

That night, we decide to all sleep out in the living room. They're both snoring away, the glow of the TV the only thing lighting up the apartment. My phone dings on the cushion next to me, and I lunge for it.

I know it's only been a few days of doing it again, but I forgot how much I hate sleeping without you, his text says. I smile.

Good thing you don't have to do it for very long. My feet are freezing. They miss you, I write back.

It dings again.

I miss you so much that I would even let you put those ice bricks on me right now. That's how much I love you, Boss.

I smile at the phone, stroking the screen like I'm touching him.

I'm glad you're mine, Waters.

We say goodnight, and I curl up on my side, Alexa's feet above my head, and Annie's head below my feet. These two became my family up here, and they always will be. Two more pieces of me that I'll carry with every step I take.

And in two weeks, after I work a few more shifts and meet with our supervisor and request my leave, I'll go back home to the man who changed my whole life the minute he walked into Andy's thirteen years ago. The man whose heart beats in sync with mine, whose breath comes from my body, whose soul is so deeply woven with my own that it's impossible to tell where one ends and the other begins.

Two bodies, one soul.

one year later

cade

"A LITTLE OVER SIXTY PERCENT."

That was what Dr. Sang had told me when I asked him what my chances of surviving were. One whole year ago.

And here I am.

"Moderate to high."

That was what he told me when I asked him what the risk was of the cancer coming back.

"Within the first two to three years."

That was what he told me when I asked him when it usually comes back, if it actually does.

But as I look down at the card that was at my spot at our table this morning, Tess's messy handwriting all over the envelope, I can't help but smile.

Happy one year of being cancer free! the outside of the homemade card reads. And on the inside, she sketched (poorly, I might add) a picture of the two of us and wrote, *and happy one year of being stuck with me. Again.*

I smile as I read it. Stuck with her sounds like

fucking heaven. I flip the card over, and I almost spit out the sip of tea I just took from the mug she left next to it.

You kicked cancer's ass, so celebrate by tapping mine!

I shake my head as I put the card back down.

I'm pretty positive my life will never, ever be dull with this woman. I hear her car pull up in the driveway of my grandfather's cabin, and I stand up and walk toward the door. I walk out onto the porch and sip my tea, watching as she gets out and walks toward me with a big white box and a smile.

"What's that?" I ask her. She smiles.

"Breakfast," she says. She gets up the stairs and opens it, and my mouth starts to water.

"No, you didn't," I say. She smiles again. "Is that—"

"Cheesecake for breakfast? Sure is," she says. "Sit down and enjoy your tea. I'll be right back with two forks. You beat cancer, you get to eat whatever the hell you want for breakfast."

I laugh and take the box from her, sitting down on one of the rocking chairs I refinished last summer. After Stevie and I sold the house last year, Tess and I bought a piece of land halfway between Grantstown and Dalesville. We officially broke ground on our house three months ago, and we're supposed to be moved in by the holidays. We come up to the cabin almost every weekend, just sitting together, smelling the trees, listening to the wind. Every weekend when we're here, I tell her to start practicing saying, 'Yes.' She pretends like she doesn't know what I'm talking about, but we both know she does.

And we both know that, someday, I'm going to make her my wife.

Sometimes, Tess still thinks I'm going to disappear. She doesn't always think I'm onto her when she gets anxious, but I am. Every time. She pulls away a bit because she's scared that I'm going to. I feel her loosen her grip on me, her mind's way of putting up a barrier, preparing for the worst.

And that's when I love her the hardest. That's when I tell her that she's going to be stuck with me for the rest of my days. *Mine.*

And slowly but surely, she comes back to me.

During the weeks, I'm back to work at the station, and I'm fucking loving it. She got a job at the hospital twenty minutes from home. The hospital where I held her when her dad died. Where I chased her around with tea in my hand. I asked her if she was sure she wanted to go back there, but she smiled and nodded.

"It's time I make new memories there," she had said. "Better ones. And when the days are tough, the best part is, I get to come home to you."

Damn right she does. Every single day. I'm the luckiest man on the whole damn planet.

Stevie and I officially divorced a few months back. Understandably, I haven't heard much from her. I'll always be grateful to her for everything she did for me, how she stuck by me, and ultimately, for what she did for Tess and me.

I talk to the moon a little less now because I roll over and just talk to Tess in bed. But when I do, I ask Grannie to find Stevie someone great. Someone who meshes with her. I ask Grannie to look out for Stevie's match.

I go back for my next six-month check up with Dr. Sang in a week. Although I'm technically in remission, I take a medication—or a "super anti-cancer pill" as I so sophisticatedly call it—that I'll be on for a few years.

I'm not naive, and neither is Tess. I know the chances of me getting this cancer again

are pretty damn good. But I'm also not the type to let my life take the lead. Instead, *I* lead my life. I refuse to go through the rest of this life scared that it might end.

I don't know how much longer I have. But the truth is, none of us do. I could stay cancer-free for the rest of my life, and someone walking around perfectly healthy right now could get hit by a bus tomorrow.

I'll never know if I lived all my life as best as I could. I'll never know if some of the choices I made were the right ones. But I do know that my life, or what's left of it, is supposed to be spent with her.

So, that's what we will do. I'll sit here on this porch of my family cabin on the outskirts of town. She'll drink her coffee. I'll drink my tea. I'll smile and watch the wind blow through her hair while she does the simplest of things.

Because that's what it's all about, isn't it? It's not all about who you want to take the adventure with. It's about who makes every day an adventure. It's about finding that person that makes it impossible to see a future without. Sometimes we lose them, sometimes we leave them, and if we're lucky, we will find our way back to them.

It's about the one that you'd look for in every life. The one you recognize from ones before this. The one you'll look for in the next. Because no matter what time, or body, or being, you belong right there with them.

Just like the stars know their place in the sky, mine is right here, next to her.

And if I leave this life before she does, I'll wait every night for that new mark on the moon.

epilogue

STEVIE

SO, what did you think?

Crazy shit, huh?

I warned you.

What a fucking *year*.

Husband gets cancer.

Husband *beats* cancer, but we end up divorced.

I know, I know. I sort of brought it on myself. I picked up that phone. I made that call. But I knew, ya know? I knew it was more than just an old friend. And even if I didn't want to face it, my gut knew. Every fiber of me knew that there was something else there.

Since we officially divorced and sold the house, obviously, people had to find out sooner or later what had happened. What I wasn't expecting were the judgments and opinions of people who had zero to do with my marriage.

You're a better person than me, because I would have XYZ. That's probably my favorite way that the passive-aggressive comments start out. I also particularly liked the ones about how I should have "beat her ass" or "kicked him to the curb, cancer or not."

Yeah, my Aunt Gretchen *actually* said that to me.

Why is it that people like to make the most comments on the subjects they know the least about?

They know nothing about the ins and outs of my marriage to Cade. They don't know how I truly did love him—and still do. About how, despite the fact that he lied to me, he was also lying to himself. He didn't mean to hurt me. He wasn't trying to break me. He was *trying* to love me.

But the truth is, even if Tess didn't exist, he never could have loved me like I should have been loved. Because while their story made it painfully clear I am not right for him, the more time I spend away from him, the more I realize, he wasn't right for me, either.

I like classical music while I clean the house. He can't stand it. I like to go out and meet new people. I like parties, and dancing, and painting. He'd prefer a quiet night in, nine times out of ten. I like small dogs. And while I loved Buster to death, it made more sense that he stayed with Cade because he was wild, and rambunctious, and not exactly the easiest to cuddle.

We're so different, Cade and I. And we did make it work. There were things we did together. But the truth is, I'm better at being apart from him than I ever was being with him.

At least, I think I am.

I'm sitting at one of the two chairs at the teeny-tiny

kitchen table in the apartment I'm renting in town. I put my two weeks in at work last week. I start a new remote job next week that pays *way* more money and lets me work in my yoga pants. Perks.

I should be looking for a place to live, a place I can buy and put my own spin on, but instead, I'm twisting the little key around between my fingers.

I'll never forget when Tess handed it to me.

It was the morning of Cade's surgery. We were in the waiting room at the hospital. We hadn't said a word all morning, but she had turned to me and pulled this key out of her bag.

"I want you to have this," she had said. I looked at her, so confused.

"Are you asking me to move in with you?" I had asked, and it brought smiles to both of our faces.

"It's a key to my Aunt Rie's cottage up in Blue Bay."

"Blue Bay?" I had asked her. She nodded.

"It's in Maine. It's nothing fancy, over a hundred years old, a two-bedroom little cottage. But it's helped me clear my head a time or two. And I just thought that if you needed a place to go at any point after all this, it might do the same for you. The address is on the tag here."

I took it from her reluctantly and had stuck it in the pocket of my purse. I thanked her and told her I'd think about it.

And it wasn't until this morning, at this table in an apartment that doesn't feel like home, when I was switching purses, that I found it again.

I think for a minute. Then, I pick up my phone.

Hey, Tess, I type, *hope all is well with you two. I wanted to let you know that if it's still okay, I'd like to go up to the Blue Bay house. I was thinking next week.*

I sit nervously at the table, chewing my thumb. I see the little dots on the screen, and I hold my breath. But a text comes in almost instantly.

Hey! I'm with my aunt now. She says it's all yours. How long you staying?

I think for a moment. Then, I type back.

Undecided.

The dots appear, then she responds.

Stay as long as you'd like to. We'll let the guy who keeps it up for us know.

Thank you, I type back. *You guys take care.*

My husband wasn't in love with me.

I know that now.

But you know what? I didn't feel like the earth was caving in when we separated. I didn't feel like I had lost a part of myself. I grieved—and still grieve—the life we had made together. But I'm surviving without him just fine. And the truth is, I was only surviving with him. I wasn't *living*. It's true what they say…that just because you're alone doesn't mean you're lonely. I've learned through all of this that the opposite can be true, too. I'm lonely now, being on my own. But I was also lonely before, when I shared a bed with someone every single night. Maybe it's because he wasn't my soulmate, if you believe in that stuff. Or maybe it's because, as much as I have tried not to admit it, I wasn't in love with myself.

And to be truthful, I'm still not completely there.

I don't know what's in Blue Bay.

I'm not sure what I'll find there.

But maybe, if I do things right, I'll find myself.

two years later

BONUS EPILOGUE

Want more of Tess and Cade's story? Sign up for my newsletter (https://bit.ly/motmbonus) and get the bonus epilogue delivered right to your email or device!

night & day duet

BOOK TWO

Ready for Stevie to get her happily ever after? Pre-order her story, Up With the Sun, now!

acknowledgments

This was the first book I wrote after almost a year-long case of writer's block. After working in healthcare during a global pandemic, my brain needed a break as much as my body did. But during that time, I learned so much about myself, and about the resilience of so many people around me.

I am forever in awe of the people who, like Tess and Cade, constantly run *toward* the fire, regardless of how big a beast it may be. I don't take the term "healthcare hero" lightly, and it was an honor to witness the strength of those people on the daily. So to all of you, thank you for showing up to the fight the fires every day, and for all you did to protect the rest of us. Specifically to my work fam, thank you for everything—the laughs, the tears, the stories, the courage—that got us through the last few years.

Krisyen & Maybe Sammi, thank you for pulling me back in and getting me back in the zone. And for answering my millions of questions, and for CONSTANTLY making me laugh. I love you both a ridicu- lous amount and couldn't be prouder of the two of you.

Cait—bless your SOUL for putting up with my inces- sant pestering, self-doubt, and all of my voice messages. You're the real MVP and I love and appreciate you SO much!

Lacey, THANK YOU for going through this with me. I'm so proud of you and grateful to call you my friend.

Jenn, thank you as always for your keen eye! I so appreciate you.

Renita, I'll never be able to thank you enough not only for dealing with me and my deadlines, but for also your endless knowledge and advice.

Lilly, B and LG — my bright spots during my dark times, the calm to every storm. I love the three of you endlessly.

about the author

T.D. Colbert is a romance and women's fiction author. When she's not chasing her kids or hanging with her husband, she's probably under her favorite blanket, either reading a book, or writing one. T.D. lives in Maryland, where she was born and raised. For more information, visit www.tdcolbert.com.

Follow T.D. on TikTok, Instagram, and on Facebook, Author T.D. Colbert, for information on upcoming books!

Are you a blogger or a reader who wants in on some secret stuff? Sign up for my newsletter, and join **TDC's VIPs** - T.D.'s reader group on Facebook for exclusive information on her next books, early cover reveals, give- aways, and more!

Made in the USA
Monee, IL
01 April 2023

31077805R00178